ONE NIGHT STAND-IN

LAUREN BLAKELY

LITTLE DOG PRESS

ALSO BY LAUREN BLAKELY

Big Rock Series

Big Rock

Mister O

Well Hung

Full Package

Joy Ride

Hard Wood

The Gift Series

The Engagement Gift

The Virgin Gift

The Decadent Gift (coming soon)

The Heartbreakers Series

Once Upon a Real Good Time

Once Upon a Sure Thing

Once Upon a Wild Fling

Boyfriend Material

Asking For a Friend

Sex and Other Shiny Objects

One Night Stand-In

Lucky In Love Series

Best Laid Plans

The Feel Good Factor

Nobody Does It Better

Unzipped

Always Satisfied Series

Satisfaction Guaranteed

Instant Gratification

Overnight Service

Never Have I Ever

Special Delivery

The Sexy Suit Series

Lucky Suit

Birthday Suit

From Paris With Love

Wanderlust

Part-Time Lover

One Love Series

The Sexy One

The Only One

The Hot One

The Knocked Up Plan

Come As You Are

Sports Romance

Most Valuable Playboy

Most Likely to Score

Standalones

Stud Finder

The V Card

The Real Deal

Unbreak My Heart

The Break-Up Album

21 Stolen Kisses

Out of Bounds

The Caught Up in Love Series:

The Swoony New Reboot of the Contemporary Romance Series

The Pretending Plot (previously called *Pretending He's Mine*)

The Dating Proposal

The Second Chance Plan (previously called *Caught Up In Us*)

The Private Rehearsal (previously called *Playing With Her Heart*)

Stars In Their Eyes Duet

My Charming Rival

My Sexy Rival

The No Regrets Series

The Thrill of It

The Start of Us

Every Second With You

The Seductive Nights Series

First Night (Julia and Clay, prequel novella)

Night After Night (Julia and Clay, book one)

After This Night (Julia and Clay, book two)

One More Night (Julia and Clay, book three)

A Wildly Seductive Night (Julia and Clay novella, book 3.5)

The Joy Delivered Duet

Nights With Him (A standalone novel about Michelle and Jack)

Forbidden Nights (A standalone novel about Nate and Casey)

The Sinful Nights Series

Sweet Sinful Nights

Sinful Desire

Sinful Longing

Sinful Love

The Fighting Fire Series

Burn For Me (Smith and Jamie)

Melt for Him (Megan and Becker)

Consumed By You (Travis and Cara)

The Jewel Series

A two-book sexy contemporary romance series

The Sapphire Affair

The Sapphire Heist

ABOUT

Lucas Xavier is the last person I want to spend 24 hours with, let alone two minutes. Exes are exes for a reason. In his case, for a million reasons. Because he's not only an ex-lover, he's also an ex-friend. We didn't just break up - we combusted in a spectacular bonfire of barbs and doors slammed.

Nothing will change that. Not his clever wit, not his ridiculous good looks, not his unfair levels of charm. And definitely not a wild dash through the city that takes us on an accidental scavenger hunt through our past, where we stop for a tango lesson, pancakes and a visit with some llamas.

And certainly not time together to make amends and say we're sorry.

But, let's say that was enough...it's not like you can fall in love in 24 hours.

ONE NIGHT STAND-IN

by Lauren Blakely

Want to be the first to learn of sales, new releases, preorders and special freebies? Sign up for my VIP mailing list here!

1
——

LOLA

I remember when a phone call used to be fun.

When your bestie would ring you after school and you'd gab for hours while snacking on Chex Mix as you pretended to tackle math problems together.

Or when the cute boy in art class would finally get the guts to dial you up and ask you to the school dance, resulting in epic squeals of happiness.

Those were the days.

Now, the phone is the enemy.

For instance, it often has the nerve to turn on the flash when I'm trying to take a surreptitious shot of a hot guy reading a paperback on the subway, something I do on behalf of all womankind—since I'm not the only red-blooded female who enjoys the hell out of that Instagram feed that posts pictures of sexy men reading in public.

Because men who read are hella hot. Because a sexy

man is a sexy man, but a sexy man who *reads*? That's like a unicorn.

Or my device often has the gall to remind me of my fitness inadequacies with its occasional notifications, like *You've only walked two miles today*, to which I say, *Fuck you, phone, I can berate myself just fine, thank you very much.*

The phone has also made it far too easy for my romance-and-intimacy lifestyle coach parents to hit me up with every *"you should try this"* opportunity under the sun.

Like, say, a couples' retreat.

A couples' date-night package.

A couples' massage.

I'm not part of a freaking couple.

Pass. Double pass. Triple bypass.

That's why I've set my phone to Do Not Disturb during my morning workout.

Plus, I don't need my phone as a distraction to survive three miles on the elliptical. I have Amy as a partner, and she's better than any TV show I'd binge while working out, especially since she's on a tangent about deep, dark secrets right this second.

"You think you know someone, Lo," she says, huffing next to me. "And then they just break out the unicycle news."

I give her a *what are you talking about* eyebrow arch, then peer at the readout—one more minute and I am finito on this sweat-till-it-hurts machine.

With her hands tightly gripped on the bars, she

shakes her head, then bites out, "My fiancé knows how to ride a unicycle. A freaking unicycle. And he didn't tell me until this weekend. We've been together for more than nine months and I am only just now learning this?"

I scoff, playing along with her indignation while I slow my pedaling. "Well, clearly that's intel he should have dropped by the third date."

"I know, right? How could Linc keep something like that from me? How could he think I wouldn't want to witness that sight with my own two eyes?"

"And when you learned of this amazing hidden talent, did you demand he show you right then and there?" I ask as I wipe my forehead with the back of my hand.

Her ponytail bobs as she nods. "Of course I did."

"And then what?" I ask as I near the blissful end of the three-hundred-calorie burner. "Wait. Let me guess. You jumped him?"

She glances at me and offers a sly little grin. "Duh."

"Gee, I wonder how I knew you'd be turned on from learning your man could ride a unicycle."

She winks. "Could it be because you know me so well?"

I hit the end button and step off the machine, my heart pounding a *thank you for working out* rhythm. Amy follows, and as we head to the locker room, my phone chirps—a tweeting sound that's one of a handful allowed through the Do Not Disturb barrier.

Those are for my best friends—Amy and Peyton—and for my clients.

Alas, Tweety signals neither Peyton nor a client.

The bird trills once more, then stops.

I groan.

Because . . . *little sisters.*

With dread, I go into the locker room and wash my hands, take ten seconds to dry them, and finish right as the phone warbles once more.

Because Luna doesn't call like a normal person.

She calls like, well, like Luna.

Rings twice, hangs up. Calls again ten seconds later.

I've told her countless times this trick is unnecessary, that my phone does this handy little thing where it blasts her name across the screen.

PITA.

Fine, that is the name I use because that's who she is.

And okay, it *does* say PITA WHO I LOVE.

Because I need the reminder.

I love this crazy girl madly, even when she plays her childhood phone games.

I slide my thumb across the screen as a half-dressed gray-haired woman in the corner of the locker room stares ice picks at me. She points to the sign near the door, stabbing the air with her finger. *No cell phone pictures. Taking a photo in a locker room is against the law.*

"I'm not taking a photo. I'm taking a call," I say to her.

Sheesh. I wasn't going to snap a shot of her for Instagram, and that's not simply because I'm not a lawbreaker. She's neither male nor reading a book. Those are the only stranger shots I take.

I motion to Amy that I'm on the phone, then I march back out into the hallway, speaking to Luna, "Kit Kat Klub. You've reached Sally Bowles. Please leave a message, and I will return your call at a *not* ungodly hour of the morning."

Giggles float across the line like bubbles blown through the summer breeze. "Lo! You're so funny. I love *Cabaret.*"

"Thank you. Please deposit fifty cents if you ever want this person to answer a call again," I say, because even though I'm wide awake, it isn't even seven. Calling at this hour should be illegal.

More laughter spills through the phone. "How do you do that? You're so fun at nine thirty in the morning," Luna says, her words gliding out like a song. I'm convinced she's a nightingale reincarnated.

She also lacks the ability to understand little things like, say, time zones.

"Luna, it's not even nine thirty where you are. You're seven hours ahead. It's . . ." I pull the phone from my ear to check the time in Athens, considering whether I can craft a voodoo doll of the phone because I can't make one of Luna. And I've tried, dear God have I ever tried. "It's one thirty where you are, and it's six thirty in New York. That's ungodly. This is a time reserved for vampires, ghosts, goblins, zombies, and New Yorkers who've adopted new workout routines and are trying to stick to them."

She gasps—such a shuddery little thing, my sister. "Lo, don't talk about zombies and vampires. You know I can't handle scary things. I didn't get your horror-loving genes. Or your morning workout drive either. But you're awake. Yay," she says, clapping. "I thought you'd be asleep."

"You thought I'd be asleep, but you called anyway?" Though the question doesn't really matter. Luna does what Luna wants. I focus on the mission-critical issues. "Are you dying, sick, in jail, in trouble, drugged, or being held captive by an alien billionaire?"

"No, God no," she says. "Those all sound horrible, even the billionaire. Besides, who needs money when you can have love instead?"

"Who said alien billionaires were incapable of love?"

"I've always thought they were."

"No. Studies have shown some species of alien billionaires have hearts," I deadpan as I stop at the water fountain for a drink. When I finish, I say, "And since you're not in custody, in a billionaire's chamber, or dead, I have to ask—is Rowan dead? I'm guessing no, because if Rowan were dead, I don't think you'd sound so happy, despite the dream you had the other night."

"Just because we had a fight before we left for the cruise doesn't mean I want him dead. I like him alive, and that's how he is right now—alive and happy next to me because we made up. I can't believe I was ever mad at him because of that silly dream. I mean, he'd never cheat in real life. But still, the dream hurt."

"Of course dream-cheating hurts," I say as sympathetically as I can, since everything hurts Luna. For all twenty-five years of her life, she's worn her heart on her sleeve.

"I'm calling for another reason," Luna says, resetting to her default cheeriness. "But don't be mad . . ."

I grit my teeth.

Oh, God. Those words would signal danger ahead for anyone, but for Luna it's more like a hurricane alert.

I lean against the cinder block of the gym hallway. "Okay, what is it this time? Because I'm *not* going to break you out of science summer camp again."

"But that was the best! Seeing all the museums in New York with you instead of making silly science fair projects—it changed my life," she says with a happy sigh. "Mom and Dad still don't know that you took me on the best field trips ever that week when they were gone."

"Not that they'd care," I say.

"Of course they'd care. That's why we kept it a secret."

No, they wouldn't. That's why I care. That's why I look out for you.

I have zero regrets about the camp breakout, on account of Luna's tumbling head over heels in love with art, but I still have to deal with this pending request and the dread crashing over me. "Is this going to be something as frustrating as that time I jimmied the lock on your storage unit to track down your good luck faux fur bolero jacket while you were on the road?"

"In my defense, I really thought I'd brought it with me, but it was the leopard-print one instead. I can't go on tours without my lucky faux fur. And it worked! The Love Birds sang to sold-out clubs. I can't ruin the luck. Luck is everything," she says.

"Don't I know it," I grumble, since luck is my sister's motto.

"But this is different. And so fun, I swear. Would I lie to you?"

"No." That much is the truth. "However, you would definitely embellish. So, bottom line . . ." I cut to the chase—whatever she needs me to do, I'll have to do it soon. Next week is huge for me. I'm competing for a book cover award at the prestigious Design-Off International, and I have a presentation to prep for the event. Not to mention my to-do list is ten feet deep and peppered with deadlines. "How much do you need for bail, and where do I post it?"

"No, it's not that crazy. It's about my landlord, Harrison," she says with a groan. "And our stuff. And this terrible letter he emailed to Rowan and me this morning. I couldn't even read the whole thing—I could barely read the first few lines. I was so upset, and I need you, Lo. I need you so much. I just can't believe he sent this email right before we're going to perform for a week. This is our big break, and he knows it. I thought he was a kindred spirit. A fellow artist who understood how hard it is to make it in this world. And to do *this*."

My brow furrows as I try to make sense of what she's saying. "To do what? What did your landlord send you a letter about?"

Her voice wobbles, and I can picture her lower lip

trembling. Classic Luna move, and it almost always works.

I am the opposite. I am iron, but I have to be with a sister like Luna. Because she's as soft as a baby duck's down.

"All my stuff," she says, her voice breaking. "I couldn't read the details through my tears, but it's about my stuff. My notebooks. My special notebooks with my song lyrics in them. And my clothes, even my plaid skirt with the special plaid buttons. And Rowan's guitars. All his precious acoustics."

I stitch on my best calm voice, the one I've used with her for years, ever since the first summer that Mom and Dad took off for a meditation retreat in the Rockies to reconnect with each other. Reconnecting with each other is pretty much all they've done since. "Where is your stuff? It's just in your apartment, right? Like, on your bureau and in the closet?"

"It's . . ." A sob floods my ears. "It's everywhere."

"Your stuff can't really be everywhere," I say, trying to soothe her. She's prone to dramatics, but even for my sister, this is a bit much.

"It is. I swear. And I need it back. We need it back. This is our big break with the Love Birds, and we have to totally focus on performing. It's not just picking it up from our place—there's actually a little more to it. The landlord went a little, well, bananas," she says.

I groan as she explains, semi-coherently, what went down. I was right to worry. This is next-level PITA.

"I don't know if I have time . . ." I say with a heavy

sigh.

"But I'll help you! Well, you'll *have* help."

I frown. "Help? Why do I need help grabbing your stuff?"

She's silent for an ominous moment. Then, in the most chipper tone of the whole damn early morning, she says, "Rowan asked Lucas to get his things."

The noisy gym goes stiller than a crypt.

The only sounds I hear are the echoes of the past, of my one-time friend.

Then Amy's sneakers squeak as she exits the locker room and heads toward me, an eyebrow cocked in curiosity.

Luna, I mouth to Amy. "You're joking," I say into the phone, forcing a calm I don't feel, clinging to a tattered hope. But secret-code phone rings aside, Luna is not a trickster.

"No. But it'll be good, right? You always liked Lucas."

"I used to like Lucas," I correct.

I used to like him a hell of a lot.

Amy's eyes widen to planet size when she hears that name. She knows the story.

Years ago, Lucas and I were friends. And then briefly, late one night, he kissed me like I was the only thing that mattered. Then *that* weekend passed, and I had to erase all my burgeoning feelings for the guy.

Now, he's my rival. A former friend. A sexy ex who didn't go back into the friendship box.

And I want to wipe that cocky smirk right off his face every damn time I see the man.

2

LUCAS

I have this theory that your behavior in a coffee shop reveals your true personality.

Spend a little time in one and you can learn everything you need to know about a person.

Does the freckle-faced redhead with the penchant for chai tea treat the corner chair as her personal den, taking phone calls from her best friend to discuss her douchey ex who she dumped three days ago but then slept with again last night?

Yes.

Yes, she does.

How about the goateed guy who's FaceTiming his roommate to discuss whether the guy on the other side of the screen Venmoed enough money to cover his portion of the extra-cheap ramen noodles they made last night? Meanwhile, goateed guy is sipping the granddaddy of expensive coffee shop concoctions—a grande latte made with espresso beans harvested by rare raccoons or something like that.

The number of things wrong with this tableau is too many to list.

Over there at a nearby table is a tattooed guy head-banging to Metallica rather than Sara Bareilles.

I'm not a big fan of either, but only one of those artists is supposed to be audible—the Sara Bareilles tunes Doctor Insomnia's coffee shop is piping through its sound system, rather than the metal screaming from the guy's headphones.

Noise-canceling for him maybe.

Not for the rest of us.

The Doctor Insomnia's owner ambles from behind the counter to ask the Metallica fan to turn it down.

I mouth *thank you* to Tommy, who gives me a *don't mention it* nod.

I return to my computer screen and the design Reid and I have been immersed in for the last two hours, fine-tuning the leaves on a book cover. He's bent over his laptop too, AirPods in. I wish I could work with music in my ears. Never been able to.

A few minutes later, the gabby redhead finishes a mind-numbing conversation about the merits of Soul-Cycle when you're back on the dating market. Her eyes swing to the restrooms, then she scans the shop.

Yup, I know what's coming.

The call-in-a-favor-from-a-stranger.

And after the morning I've had, I am not in the mood.

I rap on the table to get my business partner's attention. He removes an AirPod as I issue my prediction. "Count of ten. She's going to ask us to watch her laptop while she goes to the restroom."

He groans under his breath. "Don't do it, Lucas. Don't say it."

"Why?"

"Because it makes you sound like a dick," he mutters.

"Maybe I am one."

"You're just in a right pissy mood because of your brother."

He's right. He's always right on this count, but I can't think about Rowan this second. "Be that as it may, if we had a dime for every time someone turned around and ' asked us to babysit a laptop . . ."

He rolls his eyes. "Yeah, yeah, yeah. You'd have enough for a couple of Metro trips, mate."

"The Metro isn't free. I'd take a MetroCard on the house."

"Yeah? How's that working out for you? Anyone paying you for the number of times a stranger's asked you to keep an eye on a piece of electronics in a café?"

"No, but asking a stranger to watch your laptop is an evolutionary litmus test. It's Darwin's way of culling men and women from the herd."

"You're a piece of work. Also, for the record, I can't decide if I wish our new office space were ready so we could work there, or if watching you lose your mind at coffee shops every day is tops as the best spectator sport ever," he says, while the woman in the corner rises, surveying the landscape of patrons once more.

And I count down.

Ten, nine, eight.

The headbanger's eyes are closed, so the redhead aims her crosshairs at the goateed guy first.

Seven, six, five.

Then an older woman with her hands full of three toddlers.

Four, three, two.

Then at us.

Two guys in dress shirts and nice jeans, with expensive computers.

One. Target acquired.

Squaring her shoulders, she makes her move, crossing the few feet to our nearby table.

"Hey there," she says, then hooks her thumb in the direction of the restroom. "You look like nice guys, so I'm hoping you can just watch my laptop for, like, a sliver of a sec while I run to the big girls' room. I drank too much chai tea."

"The hazards of coffee shops," I deadpan, right as Reid cuts in, saying, "Absolutely."

She blinks, not sure who's answering her or who to talk to.

"So you'll do it?" she asks, her expression bordering on desperate.

"Happy to," Reid says.

"Nope," I say in unison.

"You're British," she says to him in a flirty tone, her lips quirking up as my friend answers her.

"I am? First I'm learning of this." He flashes her a smile, turning on the charm.

"I love British accents," she says, grinning right back at him.

"What do you know? I come fully equipped with one."

"What else do you come fully equipped with?" she purrs.

If Reid were truly flirting, I'd feel like an asshole for doing this. But I know this guy—he's not on the market.

"Question though," I say to the woman, who's demonstrated all the facets of coffee shop douchery while we've worked here on our project the last week. "How do you know *we* won't steal your laptop during that '*sliver of a sec*'? What makes you think we're nice guys? Is it his accent? Or my smile?" I give her my best *I'm a dick* grin.

"Now, now, Lucas. That's not true. Only one of us is a nice guy," Reid says to the woman, as he pats his chest and mouths, *I am.*

"In that case . . ." She stammers, then lunges several feet to her table, grabs her laptop, and clutches it to her chest. "I'll just take it with me."

"Good plan," I say, nodding my approval.

"Asshole," she mutters as she rushes to the restroom.

I turn back to the screen, but Reid is staring at me, jaw agape.

"Seriously? She was flirting with me. That was my

chance. My golden chance. *Fully equipped.* I am indeed fully equipped, and I'm happy to show her how the equipment fully works. Not to mention she's the first pretty woman to ask us to babysit a computer in the last week."

"But how does she know I'm not a hacker? A thief? Head of a black-market ring of stolen laptops and the credit cards auto-filled on them? I'm doing the world a service by saying no to those requests, even if it makes me look like a dick." I tap my temple. "I'm making her think next time she asks someone she doesn't know to watch an expensive machine." I smile proudly. "I'm rather helpful, you see."

He huffs. "Oh, right. You're a brand-new vigilante do-gooder. Captain No. Saving the world by refusing to let people be stupid."

"Captain No. I like the sound of that."

He rolls his eyes. "Because that's precisely what the world needs. We've been sorely lacking in Stupidity Police."

I preen. "Thank you. I should note that my efforts served a double purpose. Not only did I save a stranger from her own poor judgment, I saved you from a poor dating choice."

Offended, Reid straightens his spine. "I can make my own poor dating choices, thank you very much."

"Not if I can help it. One, you don't need to babysit a hot babe's laptop to get laid. Two, you're not interested, man."

"Who says I'm not interested?"

I roll my eyes. "You act like you're interested in dating, but all you do is window-shop. You're still hung up on that girl you met three years ago in Paris."

He groans, shaking his head. "I am *not* hung up."

"Tell that to the jury. Also, that woman was *not* going to give you her digits for watching her MacBook. I heard the things she was saying to her friend, or whoever it was, while you were lost in your Taylor Swift mix. You'd have taken her out for three pricey dinners and she'd still have gotten back together with her douchey ex."

"There is nothing wrong with Taylor Swift."

A smile tugs at my lips. "Funny how that's what you've glommed on to. Which proves my point again about you being hung up. And did I say there was anything wrong with Taylor?"

"You sounded like you were going to."

I give him a sympathetic smile. "Aww, you're sensitive."

"You're not," he fires back as he drags a hand through his dark hair.

"Exactly. Someone has to look out for you. And someone has to look out for my fucking kid brother."

"The truth comes out," he says with a knowing stare. "This isn't about me. Or *her*. This isn't even about your utter disdain for people who dare to break your rules of coffee shop decorum." Reid takes a beat and points at me. "This is about Rowan and the text exchange you grumbled about more than an hour ago."

I groan from the black depths of my soul. "I love that

kid, but seriously. What the hell am I going to do with him?"

"Well, he *is* an adult."

"He's twenty-five going on eight," I say, as evidenced by his messages this morning.

"You could say no," Reid offers.

My shoulders sag as I briefly consider that tempting possibility.

But there is no *no*.

I can't say no to the knucklehead, even though I want to.

Lord knows how desperately I want to, especially as I pick up my phone and reread his texts from an hour ago.

Rowan: Hey!

Rowan: How the hell are you?

Rowan: Is business good?

Rowan: Are you still kicking ass as New York's top graphic designer?

Rowan: I bet you've won ten more awards since the last time we spoke. Nabbed twenty more clients. Wiped the floor with the competition.

Rowan: Because you, my big bro, are a rock star.

Did he think I couldn't read between the lines? When Rowan goes into full fluffer mode, he's going in for the big favor.

And that's what he asked for. I grit my teeth as I read the next text, the very note that ignited my fine mood.

Rowan: So, listen. I need you to do me a solid. Our landlord is a total drama llama. I swear, he's just jelly that Luna and I are landing some stellar gigs. And he threw out all our stuff because of what went down the last night we were in town. But seriously, what's the biggie? We are a fiery couple, and sometimes we have tiffs.

Lucas: You and Luna have tiffs like Mike Tyson has tiffs.

Rowan: Please. I never bit her ear off.

Lucas: Not yet.

Rowan: Anyway, we're here in Athens (and we are madly in love still!), but we're about to go dark for, like, eight days because of this Mediterranean cruise. (Which is fully booked! And I can't wait to croon my heart out with my girl all night long on the club level! Love Birds indeed!) So . . . if you can help your little bro out and get my stuff, that would be awesome. I owe you big-time, and I love you, man.

Lucas: What do you need?

Rowan: Just a couple things. I need my guitars for this auction coming up for the children's hospital, and my clothes, obvs, and my collection of Star Wars T-shirts, which are my good luck charm, and since I don't have them, that's obviously why Luna and I were fighting.

Lucas: That's more than a couple things, Rowan.

Rowan: I know, I know! But please be my Obi-Wan. You're my only hope.

Lucas: Fine. But because of the Star Wars T-shirts. That I understand. Well, not the Star Wars obsession, but the T-shirt one. Where do I get your stuff from? Your place? I assume the key still works?

Rowan: Well, that's the funny thing . . .

I set the phone down and take a fueling drink of my coffee. I need another hit of caffeine before I reread his last text. Because I don't have time for a scavenger hunt. Not when I have clients breathing down my neck, not with the design competition in sight. Nabbing the top prize with a killer presentation would be huge for our firm, and I don't need a single distraction.

I meet Reid's *I told you so* gaze, feeling sheepish as I gesture to the string of texts. "Look, I can't say no to Rowan." I wince. "Not least because I already said yes."

He shakes his head. "You always say yes to him. Like that time you had to proof his history paper. He was a senior in college."

"He's bad with grammar!"

"So is nearly everyone. But hey, you can take up that cause too. Be a grammar cop."

I shoot him a sharp look. "No one, not even I, has time for that."

Reid leans back in his chair and strokes his chin. "Or what about last year when he performed in Colorado? Remember how he called you and said, 'Dude, my hands are so dry I can't play my guitar'?"

"Yes," I mutter, knowing what's coming next.

"You told him to go to the store and get hand lotion, and he said he didn't know what kind and it was too confusing and he was just wandering the aisles not knowing what to buy."

I scrub my hand across my chin, looking away.

"And what did you do?" he continues like a prosecutor.

I glance at the headbanger, who's now air drumming. I wish I had massive headphones on right now. I wish my hearing were noise-canceling.

"I called the store and told the store manager what kind to put aside for him," I grumble.

Reid's lips twitch in a victory grin. "But that's not all." He wiggles his fingers. "Serve it up. Every detail."

"I paid for it for him," I blurt out. "There. Are you happy?"

He crosses his arms, grinning. "A little bit. Now, tell me again why you said yes to this new request?"

I heave a frustrated sigh. "It's fine. It'll be easy. How long can it possibly take to gather his things? He hasn't forwarded me the email from his landlord with all the details yet, but it'll take maybe a day, tops."

"A day you don't entirely have to spare."

"Then I'll make a deal with the landlord and buy him off."

He arches a dubious brow. "Do you hear what you're saying?"

"I do."

"And you realize you're thinking of paying off a landlord to help your twenty-five-year-old brother?"

I wave a hand dismissively. Reid doesn't know the half of it. Helping Rowan is what I do. It's what I've always done. Because somebody has to. "It's not a big deal," I insist.

"Maybe not this time. But perhaps next time he asks you for a favor, consider saying no. You do it so well with strangers. Try it with family." He demonstrates, nodding at an imaginary person. "Thanks, but no thanks." Then another. "Appreciate the offer, but I have to decline." Then one more. "No fucking way. I will not pick up your stuff all over Brooklyn, and if you'd have asked me to watch your laptop, that would have been a 'hell no' too, complete with a spank for being stupid."

I roll my eyes. "And on that note, I'm going back to work, since tonight I'll have to collect his things."

But before I can wake up my laptop, the redhead exits the restroom and marches straight over to me.

"You're not only an asshole—you're an arrogant asshole." Then she leans in close to Reid, getting in his face. "And for the record, I *was* going to give you my number."

Reid blinks, called on his bullshit.

Then she adds, "*Fake digits.* I was going to give you fake digits. I heard you singing along to Taylor Swift, so I figured you were harmless."

He scoffs. "There is nothing wrong with Taylor Swift. Also, I didn't want your digits," he shouts as she storms out the door, laptop tucked under her arm.

I hold my hands up in surrender. "See? It all worked out for the best."

We return to work. But a few seconds later, my phone bleats loudly.

My brother. What does he want now?

I hit mute so it doesn't ring again, then tell Reid I'll take the call outside.

"Who's going to watch your laptop?" Reid asks innocently. "Taylor Swift?"

"You are, because I saved you from that woman," I say, then dart outside and answer the call. "What's going on?"

"Not much," Rowan says, with a laugh that sounds forced. "Everything is great."

My hackles go up. "Let me ask again. What's going on now?"

Rowan clears his throat. "Listen, it's no biggie. Everything is cool. I mean, it will be when we get our stuff back, plus the security deposit, which we're totally going to need. Anyway, I just sent you the email with the details. But there's one little thing I forgot to tell you, and I need to let you know now before we board this cruise."

I groan. "Your stuff isn't in Brooklyn?"

"No. It probably is. I mean, that'd make sense. I'd have to look at the email more closely to know for sure, and I didn't read it yet because it was super long and annoying and messing with my mojo. But that's not the point."

A ship's horn cuts through his voice, and I can't hear a word he's saying. When the horn ends, he says, "So, you don't mind, do you?"

"Mind what?" I ask, my jaw ticking as the May sunshine dares to peek out from behind a cloud. It should be raining. It should be fucking pouring right now.

"You don't mind that Luna asked for help too?"

I let out a sigh of relief. "No, that's fine, of course. It'll be done faster then," I say before I connect the dots. But when I do, all the life leaks out of me. I brace myself for an answer I don't want. But I have to ask the question. "Who's helping Luna? Is it her sister?"

Please say no. Please say no.

I can hear Rowan smile as he answers, "Yes. Lola will help."

Lola Dumont.

Lola *fucking* Dumont.

I lean against the coffee shop's brick wall, picturing the last time I saw the dark-haired beauty at an industry event. She'd looked like she wanted to toss her champagne at me. Then deliver a scathing rebuttal listing all my mistakes.

Hell, there were things I wanted to say to her too.

When her name pops up in my texts a few minutes later, my brain plays a cruel joke by reminding me of three things.

How much fun we had together for that one year when we were nearly inseparable.

How good her lips tasted the night I kissed her.

And how shitty I felt the weekend *after*.

3

LOLA

Isn't a morning workout supposed to de-stress you?

That's why I started my new regimen—begin the day right, and all that jazz. Though, credit where credit's due, the early-bird fitness strategy was Amy's idea. She twisted my arm a month ago. "If I'm going to enter the endurance sport of wedding cake testing, I need to adopt a new workout ritual. And pretty please, will you be my fitness partner at the crack of dawn?"

I'd said yes instantly, because my two shrinks—aka my good friends Peyton and Amy—keep telling me I need less stress in my life.

Sure, the stress is technically self-induced because I just branched out on my own. Starting a business is both a wonderful and terrifying adventure.

I used to be a staff designer at the Bailey & Brooks publishing house, but I've always wanted to run my own design firm. In the last year, I took the first few steps, finagling a contractor position here at the publishing house, cutting down my time to three days a week. The other two days are for me to develop my own clients, and I've nabbed a handful so far—clients I need to tend to both tonight and this weekend, because that's how you build a business.

Round the freaking clock.

But now, I have unexpected plans. The giant flat tire of picking up my sister's stuff from all over Brooklyn.

When she forwards the email, she sends along a series of text messages strewn with stars and comets. That tugs at my stupid heart—it's our code. Our sister language. And it's exactly why I'm doing this for her. This touring opportunity is her dream, and if picking up her crap helps her, I'll do it.

I reply with a moon, and she writes back with the sun. Then she says she's about to lose cell service, but she loves me with all her heart and soul.

And I love her too.

After I shower, tame my dark curls into an acceptable mane, and dress for work, Amy and I leave the gym. On the walk to Bailey & Brooks, where Amy is a full-time kick-ass editor, we dissect the world's most ridiculous email.

"It figures that my sister would have a dramatic landlord," I say as we turn down Madison Avenue.

"Like attracts like?" Amy offers.

A flash of silver streaks by on the busy street. I jerk

my head toward the spandexed rollerblader cruising the streets at the speed of an Italian race car. A former rollerblading champion, he's hell-bent on restoring the sport to its 1990s glory days with his YouTube channel.

"Hi, Peter," I shout.

The fortysomething man angles up his purple Rollerblade, slamming on the brake. Hopping onto the sidewalk, he wheels over to us, whipping off his gleaming black helmet with its GoPro camera mounted to the front. "Lola! Are we still on for coffee this evening? To review the graphics?"

I wince, then give him my best professional smile. "Any chance we can switch to tomorrow morning? Coffee's best in the morning anyway."

He pouts, like he's so put out, then he shrugs happily. "If you insist. Gives me more twilight blading time anyway."

"And that's what matters most. I'll have everything ready to show you in the morning," I say. He gives me a thumbs-up then Froggers his way across the avenue, attacking the street once more with his trademark ferocity.

Amy nudges me. "For the record, I love that your first client is none other than Peter the Blade. Maybe he'll even write a memoir someday of his wild rollerblading exploits and you can design an awesome book cover for it, thus bringing your professional worlds full circle."

"Yes, and designing that, or anything for that matter, would be so much more fun than picking up my sister's stuff," I say as I return to the issue at hand, shaking my phone at the sky as we near our skyscraper. "What kind of landlord sends a message like this? A deranged one, clearly."

When we enter the revolving glass doors, Amy taps her chin thoughtfully. "Are we sure the landlord is a wackadoodle?"

I roll my eyes. "What else could he be?"

Amy scrunches up her brow, deep in thought. "Last time we went out with your sister, didn't she say the landlord was an aspiring TV writer?"

That sounds familiar. I swipe my ID card through the security turnstiles in the lobby, Amy following behind me. "Luna said she'd thought he was a kindred spirit. A fellow artist. But how does that explain this email?"

Amy's green eyes twinkle. "Because there's something more to this *breakup letter*. He's not simply peeved. He's *delightfully* peeved. I bet he's writing a TV pilot. Like, for a caper." She rubs her palms together. "Maybe he's testing out concepts."

I groan. "Great. So I could be a pawn in a wackadoodle's writing experiment."

"Writers are weird. Basically, everything around them is fodder. Put yourself on a writer's bad side, and you're the next victim in a murder mystery."

I shudder. "Can he please be writing a children's show instead in this scenario?"

"You might be a giant purple dinosaur then, so be careful what you wish for." She taps her chin as we wait

for the elevator. They take forever in the mornings.
"Read me the email again."

To: Luna Dumont, Rowan Xavier
From: Harrison Bates
Subject: Let's Break Up Early!

Dear Luna and Rowan,

They say all good things come to an end.

And they are right.

Slices of pizza from Famous Ray's don't go on forever,
nor do vacations, Sundays, or TV shows like *The Office*.

My point is this.

Your lease is up in exactly one month. (By the way, feel
free to check the fine print—I did, many times, while
you two were arguing over the indignity of Luna
watching the new *Aladdin* before you saw it, Rowan. So
what? So she went to the movies without you. You
survived! Also, we all know how the story ends.
Happily! Freaking happily ever after.
Sheesh. It's a fairy tale, for crying out loud.)

(And Luna, while we're splitting hairs, GIF is
pronounced with a soft *G*. Like the brand of peanut

butter. Like, you know, how the inventor of the format says it's pronounced. I sided with Rowan on that argument you two had at three in the morning when I was trying to sleep before I had a very important meeting the next morning about a very important project that turned into a very big rejection because I'd had very little shut-eye. But enough about me.)

You two angry lovebirds are in violation of a certain clause. In the event of ongoing excessive noise (aka earsplitting, sky-rending DRAMA!), this lease can be terminated at any point.

There you go!

It's over.

Finito.

We're done.

We are never getting back together.

But don't worry, I didn't break your things, like you broke my eardrums with your nightly arguments! (Also, Rowan, on behalf of all the men in the world, I commend you for holding your ground the other night on the dream-cheating. We need men to pave the path on this issue, but not necessarily at top volume.)

Anyway, because I'm thoughtful, I packed your things! And I even invented a neat game, since I know you like playing games! (And please, for the love of board games, Rowan, have a little class—don't buy a property you don't need in Monopoly. Everyone in the building heard you two quibbling over this with your mega-phonic voices. Every single tenant. And we all know the gentleman's rule of Monopoly—don't be a property pig. And Luna, don't skim so many hundreds from the bank. That's just all kinds of wrong.)

Without further ado, here's where you'll find your stuff:

- Let's start with an easy one. Your guitars are where you first met!
- Or maybe it's not so easy. Because your Star Wars T-shirts are where you argued over where you first met! Hint: there was cheese involved, you little hipsters.
- Remember that debate over who was better at leading and who was better at following? You had it the night you took a certain class. You'll find your iPad there.
- Your songwriting notebooks are where you had the "Oh my God, wasn't that the hottest makeup sex ever, babe?" and "The only thing that would have made it hotter would have been syrup." Hint: you were making up

following an epic nine rounds over whether
or not *Die Hard* is a Christmas movie!

- Your clothes are evenly split among the places
where you each dragged the other to prove
who had a better plan for how to spend
hypothetical lottery winnings.

If you find everything within forty-eight hours, I'll give
you back your security deposit! You'll need it, I
suspect, based on all the times you argued over who
was paying for the quinoa kale tofu burgers you'd just
bought.

Have fun! Oh, and while I didn't break or damage
anything, I can't guarantee anybody else won't find it
first! Ticktock.

My best,
Harrison

P.S. *Die Hard* is definitely a Christmas movie.

I finish the note as the elevator reaches our floor and
the doors slide open. Amy tucks a few strands of hair

behind her ears, then declares, "Definitely a writer. He's absolutely a quirky TV writer."

"He's a sadist. A sick, twisted sadist," I say as we pass the receptionist desk, waving hello to Zoe.

Amy lifts a brow at me. "Is there any other kind of sadist?"

"Like a gleeful sadist? A happy-go-lucky sadist?" I offer.

Her green eyes sparkle. "*The Happy-Go-Lucky Sadist.* Perfect title for a new TV pilot."

"I'm sure Webflix will pick it up." I pause and dramatically sweep my arm to an invisible spectacle, turning on my movie trailer voice. "*Binge-watch The Happy-Go-Lucky Sadist, a new dark comedy about a landlord with a vengeance.* Insert dramatic pause. *A vengeance for hijinks.*"

Amy laughs, swiping strands of brunette hair from her cheek as we continue our pace. "I'm so there for it. I'll make the popcorn."

"I'll bring the wine." I turn down the hall toward my office. "Except. Wait. I'm wrong. My sister and her boyfriend are the true sadists. For making me do this with Lucas, the ex who never apologized."

"That is definitely grounds for admission to the sadists club." Amy pats my shoulder. "I can still hate Lucas for you if you want me to. Should I keep him in the permanent hate database?"

I wave a hand airily. "He's not worth it. He wasn't worth it all those years ago when he ditched me for our first date, after a year of friendship, and he's not worth it now."

Even though I'd have thought a year of friendship would've meant something to him. I bite back those words. I honestly don't even care about what happened between us back then or his silly excuses. I've let it go. But Lucas still finds it necessary to needle me every time we run into each other. My jaw tightens as I picture the evening ahead. It used to be so easy to spend time with him. Hanging out with him—in museums, in dorm lounges, in New York City cafés—had been the recipe for a good day, and all our days were good. Now? Nothing's the same.

"Maybe I should reach out to the sadist and try to talk some sense into him?"

Amy shoots me a doubtful look. "Sure, give it your best shot. But my money says someone who goes to this much trouble to write that note and plant all those belongings isn't going to be deterred by sweet talk."

I consider this, and the truth is she's probably right. "Then I'm going to focus on working efficiently and cordially with Lucas to power my way through this list and be done with it."

"That's the spirit." She winks. "Be cordial with the sexy ex. I've seen his picture. He's definitely danger-ously good-looking."

I stare at her like she's in big trouble. "Thanks for reminding me he's too hot for words. Maybe you're the sadist."

She wiggles her brows before she heads to her office

to, presumably, work on refining a pitch for *The Happy-Go-Lucky Sadist* concept.

When I reach my three-days-a-week desk, I dive in.

I google Harrison Bates.

But all I find is bare bones info. He owns a building in Brooklyn. He has a brother. If I pay fifty-four dollars, some company will unlock his phone number for me.

There isn't much more on him, and kudos to the guy for living a life off social media.

Still, it's time to tackle this shit show.

4

LOLA

I give it my best college try, tapping out an email to the landlord and hitting send.

To: Harrison Bates
From: Lola Dumont
Subject: FW: Let's Break Up Early!

Hi there, Harrison!

How are you? I hope this email finds you well. I'm Luna's sister, and I understand you're frustrated with her and Rowan. Is there any chance we can talk about perhaps an easier way for me to retrieve their items? Since she's out of town and all.

I look forward to hearing back.

My best,
Lola

To: Lola Dumont
From: Harrison Bates
Subject: Re: FW: Let's Break Up Early!

Sure! The easier way is to wait for her to come back and then Loudmouth and Louder-mouth can do it themselves! And then they'll lose their security deposit! Also, that's super nice of you to do it for them. If you get it back, they should give you their security deposit as a thanks!

Harrison

I groan, then find the sexy ex's—I mean Lucas's—phone number on the email from my sadistic sister and send him a text.

* * *

Lola: I have one day to devote to this sibling assignment. I'll meet you at their place tonight at seven.

Lucas: Whoa. How about a "Hello? How are you? How have you been, my old friend?"

Lola: Are you really going to correct my social graces at this particular moment? Also, "*old friend*"? Revisionist historian, much?

Lucas: My memory is irrefutable. There was definitely friendship before you smothered it.

Lola: Ah, yes. I was the sole one responsible for the smothering. You had nothing to do with it.

Lucas: See? My point exactly. But enough about the past. I was hoping you'd at the very least try to ply me with dinner and drinks before you attempted to get me in bed at your sister's place.

Lola: If I were trying to get you in bed—something that wouldn't even happen as a way to pass the time during a zombie apocalypse—such a tryst would never occur in my sister's bed.

Lucas: Ah, my mistake. You did say we should meet at their place, so I presumed you wanted to have your way with me. I guess another reason might be to try to negotiate with Mr. Bates. Perhaps you'll have better luck. I attempted to rationalize with him.

Lola: And how did those efforts go?

Lucas: I would say *"not well"* is a fair way to describe them. But I'll screenshot them so you can see for yourself. Here you go.

* * *

To: Harrison Bates
From: Lucas Xavier
Subject: FW: Let's Break Up Early!

Hey,

This is Rowan's brother. Let's cut to the chase and put this mess behind us. What do you need to just hand over their stuff and move on?

Lucas

To: Lucas Xavier
From: Harrison Bates
Subject: Re: FW: Let's Break Up Early!

Hello Lucas!

I'd have to check my running tab of time lost, creativity sapped, and weeks of writer's block on account of Loudmouth and Louder-mouth. Hold on.

Be right back . . .

Okay! I calculated it.

How's $5679?

If that works for you, it's good with me! Otherwise, have fun! That's all this is—just some fun and games.

Harrison

To: Harrison Bates
From: Lucas Xavier
Subject: Re: Re: FW: Let's Break Up Early!

Sounds more like payback. And the answer is no.

To: Lucas Xavier
From: Harrison Bates
Subject: Re: Re: Re: FW: Let's Break Up Early!

But payback can be fun for all parties involved. I swear!

* * *

Gobsmacked, I stare at the screenshot. Amy was right—Harrison is *delightfully* peeved. Wait. Make that *gleefully*. I slump in my chair, groaning. "Luna, what have you gotten me into?"

But there's no time to wallow. The sooner I handle my sister's mess, the sooner I can put it in the rearview mirror.

I tap out a reply to Lucas, lest he think he's the only one who searched for an alternative.

Lola: I reached out to him as well and was similarly rebuffed.

Lucas: As you can see, I took the liberty of rebuffing his offer. But if you want to fork over some green, feel free. (Also, to your point about trying to get me between the sheets, I assure you, bed with me is an excellent way to pass the time, zombie apocalypse or not.)

Lola: Let me go ahead and file that under things that will never happen. And just to be 100 percent clear—something that may confound you—I suggested meeting at their place to go through the list, not to bed you. Let's focus on the task and get it done.

Lucas: Was it really a suggestion though? Seemed more like an order. But I can get on board with orders.

Lola: The list, Lucas. Let's meet at their place to go over this godforsaken, demented list.

Lucas: Sure, it's all about the list. Wink, wink. If you say so.

Lola: You are and always have been exasperating. Now, Mr. Social Graces Police, please do let me know if seven p.m. works for you?

Lucas: If it works for you, sweetheart, I'm there.

Lola: Yes. But don't call me "sweetheart."

Lucas: Is "darling" better? You don't seem like a "darling," but hey, if that's what you're into now, so be it.

Lola: I am into helping my sister. I will see you tonight.

I shove my phone into a drawer, turning the traitorous device to silent, in case that man attempts to distract me with another infuriating text.

Wait. Screw that. I refuse to be distracted by . . . *pseudo exes.*

That's what he is.

He's barely even an ex.

He's a quasi ex.

And every smart, modern, educated woman in the

city knows you don't give an ounce of energy to quasi exes from college.

I draw a deep breath, trying to channel some of my morning workout endorphins to fuel me all day long.

I'm nose to the grindstone for the next eight hours. I stop briefly to have a quick deskside lunch with my friend Baldwin, an editor here.

"Listen, pretty lady, I need to know if I should wear the pinstriped T-shirt when I take James to the Yankees game this weekend, or if I should wear this gray one, which admittedly makes me look pretty edible," he says, showing me the options on his phone.

"Definitely the gray one."

He winks as we finish our salads. "Always good advice to look edible."

We finish and I return to my computer screen, barely glancing away except for one brief lightbulb-flashing moment when I cackle out loud like an evil genius. At the end of the day, I pop into Amy's office to say goodbye.

"Wish I was joining you and Peyton at Gin Joint," I say with a pout.

"*Le sigh*. Me too. But with your brainpower, I bet you'll have all the items back in a few hours, and then you can put this list behind you."

I knock on wood, though I'm not superstitious. That's Luna's department. We're both artsy, but we're on opposite ends. She's the head-in-the-clouds sister; I'm the get-shit-done one. "And once it's behind me, I can focus on the design competition. Which brings me to my crackerjack plan," I say, wiggling my eyebrows.

"I love it already," she says before I can breathe a word. "But now, tell me everything."

"Lucas's design was short-listed for the Design-Off International. So, this scavenger hunt will serve a double purpose. Retrieve Luna's things and scope out the competition."

Amy nods approvingly. "I love when you talk spy. Go get 'em, Double-O-Seven."

"I will," I say, then head home to spend a half-hour on Peter's designs—I'm adding some slick graphic elements to snaz up his YouTube channel. Confident he'll like these, I save the files, back them up in my Dropbox, then confirm a time for our meeting in the morning.

I shower and change into skinny jeans, ankle boots, and a form-fitting black T-shirt. One that happens to have a V-neck.

That might also be a little snug.

That possibly makes me look like a babe, as my last beau, Fabian, declared when he saw me in it. But that was before Fabian turned into a stage-five clinger, and this modern woman doesn't have time for clingers or for relationships.

So I said goodbye to Fabian, sending him the way of Alejandro and the others. But even though I'm wearing man blinders these days, I can definitely wedge in a little taunting of a quasi ex in the form of a sexy-casual ensemble.

After all, it can't hurt for Lucas to remember what he missed out on that weekend in college.

Me.

He missed out on me.

Even though his excuse was lame, I did understand how he missed our first date. The issue wasn't the *why*. It was the lack of a true apology. I didn't need to get involved with a man who couldn't find it in himself to say he was truly sorry for what happened that weekend. I made it easier for both of us by saying, *We should just go back to being friends.*

Only, we became rivals instead, competing for coveted undergrad assignments, internships, and awards.

I leave my place in Chelsea, pop in my AirPods to tune in to a new podcast drama about a cursed carnival and the eerie enchantments that occur in it at night, and catch the subway to Brooklyn.

When I exit the train in Prospect Park and wind through my sister's neighborhood, I find my ersatz ex lounging on the steps of my sister's building, his long, athletic frame stretched out ever so casually, the fading sun casting a sunset glow on his carved cheekbones.

Damn those cheekbones.

Screw that square jaw.

And carnival curse those broody brown eyes.

He's both an artist and an athlete, just like he was in college.

But when I take in his dark jeans, his T-shirt with a stick figure on it, and the five-o'clock stubble that graces his olive skin, I have a feeling he dipped his hand into the same bag of tricks I did.

The "tempt the old flame" one.

Because that man, does he ever look fine.

I have no choice but to pretend I'm made of ice.

5

LUCAS

"Hi. We don't have time to sit. We have less than forty-eight hours," she says, all *chop-chop* without so much as a proper hello.

This woman. The look she fires at me could freeze a dick in a Rio de Janeiro summer. A dick on a beach staring at babes in bikinis.

Did I dodge a bullet in college or what?

Someone was looking out for me then.

Maybe I had some regrets at the time. Maybe I wished I'd handled it differently. But right now, with her icicle eyes, I'm all good with how shit went down.

Even so, I need to lock down my reaction to her. But with her wearing those painted-on jeans and that snug-as-sin shirt that shows off the hollow of her throat and the curves of her breasts, resistance is as hard as stone.

Be casual. Don't think with your little head this time.

I stretch my arms up high, taking my time answering the ice queen, trying to shake off my inconvenient lust.

"True, we do have only two days, but I'm pretty sure you said you're devoting one mere day to the cause. That's what you said in your text. So, looks like we have twenty-four hours. But don't worry. I know math is hard." I give her a sympathetic smile.

She rolls her chocolate-brown eyes, then adopts a plastic grin. "Yes, and it's been typically challenging for you too. Differentiating between a weekend and a day was never your strong suit."

Sighing heavily, I stand. What's the point in arguing with her? We hashed out this little *was it a day, was it a weekend* issue back when my lacrosse team captains decided to steal the team away for a weekend instead of an afternoon.

The timing sucked.

The night before, Lola and I had been hanging out, as we often did. That night, though, hanging out had turned into a soft and tender kiss, which had turned into a hot and heavy kiss, which had turned into something more as she fell apart beneath my fingers.

And that turned into me asking, *Can I take you to the department dinner on Saturday night?*

The one with all the professors?

Yes.

With delight in her pretty brown eyes, she'd said, I'd love to go with you.

Then Saturday came, and my teammates showed up at my door and said they were taking us away for the afternoon for team bonding, no phones allowed.

The afternoon turned out to be the whole weekend.

The net result? Technically, I stood her up. I wasn't able to make what would have been our first official date, and I'd had no way of reaching her.

I'd felt like complete and utter shit. But when I returned and tried to explain what happened—the captains kidnapping us, the camping and fishing trip—well, Lola said it was no big deal and that we were better off as friends anyway.

Okayyyyyy.

Hell if I was going to let on that I was hurt. Or that I wanted to make it up to her, to take her out again and properly say I was sorry.

No fucking way.

If she wanted to friend-zone me, I wasn't going to fight for more. *Fine*, I'd said. *It was just one night anyway.*

Yeah, that comment didn't go over so well. But hey, we were going to be friends again and our friendship could withstand a little awkward moment.

Only, we weren't a rubber band that snapped back into friendship shape.

We are *this*—the older brother and sister of a pair of crazy young lovers, and also rivals in business. Even more so now with the design competition next week.

I point to my watch. "As the man himself said, tick-tock. What do you want to tackle first?"

"The first item, I presume." Reaching into her back pocket, she grabs her phone, taps on the screen, then scrolls.

But I don't need to look up the email. I remember it.

"If memory serves, the email from the Ringmaster listed where they first met as item *numero uno*," I say.

She glances up from the phone, the corner of her lips quirking. "'Ringmaster,'" she says, like she's testing the word on her tongue. "That works. Though personally I like to call him 'The Happy-Go-Lucky Sadist.'"

I scrub a hand across my chin, considering this nickname. It's not bad. Not bad at all. But I can't give an inch to this woman. She is a ferocious tiger, and she'll pounce. Like she did when I ran into her at an industry conference a year ago. Checking out the paperback jacket on display at one of the booths, she'd said my design for the memoir *If Found, Please Return* was a top candidate for the new award category Imitation Is the Sincerest Form of Flattery, since she claimed it was the spitting image of a cover from another publishing house.

My cover had released first, I pointed out. Then I told her that her cover for *Fashion Roadkill* looked like it was drawn by a pigeon on speed.

That was a red-hot lie. That cover was earth-shatteringly good.

"I'll stick to 'Ringmaster,'" I say, furrowing my brow as I laser in on the mission. Trouble is, I've been noodling on the first item all day, but I'm not positive where my brother and his girlfriend met. Hell, does Rowan even know? Doubtful. But I bet Lola knows, since that's the type of stuff girls gab about. "So, do you know where Luna and Rowan met?"

"Of course I do." She parks a hand on her hip, like the answer is so obvious. "The Cute As A store."

I lift a doubtful brow. "What are you talking about? What store?"

She huffs, flapping her arms, pointing down the tree-lined street. "It's ten blocks away. The button shop," she says, taking a beat like she's waiting for me to connect the dots. But the dots remain disconnected. "As in, 'cute as a button.' Luna was hunting for a new plaid dot button to go with her good-luck plaid skirt, and Rowan needed one for his Anakin Skywalker costume for a party he was going to. A Halloween party."

I blink, shaking my head like I can clear the ridiculous from it, though it's hard to know where to begin sorting out that infodump. I start at square one. "Is there actually a store called Cute As A instead of Cute As A Button?"

She laughs lightly, the gold flecks in her eyes twinkling as she does. "It's a pretty bad one as far as names go."

I gesture to the sidewalk in the direction of the store. "I'd say it's officially trying too hard."

"Right? No one knows what it is when you first say it. You always have to fill in the gap," she says as we walk past the brownstones then a gourmet mustard shop tucked between two buildings. "Just call it what it is, right?"

"There is definitely way too much let's-try-to-be-clever going on in this world. Like specialty mustard shops."

"And toe-ring stores," she adds.

I swivel around, scanning for such an offensive jewelry boutique. "Please tell me there is no such thing."

She snaps her gaze to me and lifts a hand like she's taking an oath. "I swear on a stack of Anne Rice novels. I actually passed a store in Soho the other day called *This Little Piggy*, and it sells all sorts of toe rings. Coral, platinum, and rose gold. They size your toes, measure them, and custom-make toe rings too."

I cringe. "I feel like I might need to unlearn everything you just said."

"Oh, trust me. I'd like to go back to the days when I was more innocent too. Alas, I've had to accept we live in a world with *This Little Piggy*. And *Mightier Than.*"

My mental wheels turn, trying to place that name, then it clicks. "The designer pencil shop? The one in Queens? With carpenter pencils? Vintage pencils? And pencil sets with all colors of the palette?"

"Don't forget you can buy an old-fashioned schoolhouse pencil sharpener there too," she says.

"How could I forget that? Especially since I'm *always* in the market for something that reminds me of elementary school," I deadpan.

"Next thing we know, there will be Play-Doh shops for adults."

I shudder. "Stop. Make it stop."

We reach a walk sign at the crosswalk, scanning left and right to make sure it's safe. "We can't make it stop. The world only spins forward, and next thing you know, the Play-Doh shops will have wine and spaghetti-hair-making classes too," she says as she steps into the street. Out of nowhere, a motorcycle whizzes toward her, hell-bent on running the light. Pulse spiking, I grab her arm, yanking her hard out of the street and smack back onto the sidewalk.

Stumbling, she slams against me, her spine to my chest as the motorcycle screeches to a stop. In a split second, my arm ropes around her waist, her body tight against mine.

Like it was that night.

The memories flood back in a rush—her scent, her sounds, her moans. How she said my name.

As I tell myself to focus, her breath catches, and she gasps. "Holy . . ."

My heart stutters, adrenaline pumping through me. "Yeah."

"Wow," she says under her breath, shuddering.

"You okay?" I ask softly, trying not to breathe in the luscious smell of her hair. She smells like a tropical sea breeze, and that is not fucking helpful. Nor is the snug way she fits against me, her curves lined up just so.

"Yes. I'm fine." She takes another deep inhale, then brushes her hands over her shirt, gently tugging away. "I didn't see him coming."

"Yeah, I didn't at first either," I say, wishing for a second that she were still sealed to me.

But that's a stupid wish, so I focus on the dickhead on the Vespa. A DoorDash bag hangs on the back of his bike, and he's tapping away on his phone. Seriously?

I cup my hands around my mouth and call out to the

asshole, "Put your phone away! You could have killed someone."

But my helpful suggestions fall on deaf ears. The light's changed again, and he's cranked the throttle on the bike, revving away.

Lola, seeming less shaken now, stares at me like I'm a dog doing a handstand.

"What?"

She points, drawing a circle to encompass me. "You're one of *those* people now?"

My brow creases. "One of what people?"

"Those people who yell at strangers," she says, smirking.

"For texting and driving and nearly killing someone? Yes. Yes, I am." I own it as we wait for the walk sign again.

"Lucas Xavier from *São Paulo*." She gives a satisfied sigh, saying my name the same way she did the first time we met in a graphic design studio class at art school, like it tastes good in her mouth.

I'm Lola Dumont from Miami, but I was raised in New York, and I want to be a great designer, she'd said.

Lucas Xavier from São Paulo, and I grew up in Connecticut, and I want to be an even better designer.

Then I guess we'll see who wins, Lucas Xavier from São Paulo.

"You always did want to save the world," she continues. "I just never thought you'd do it this way."

"And what is that supposed to mean?"

"You know what I mean. You were the king of causes

in college. You were always taking up rallying cries. *Free speech. Recycle more. Save the forests.*"

"Those are all good causes." To make my point, I grab an empty water bottle from the sidewalk and drop it with panache into a recycling bin at the corner. I wait for the satisfying *thwap* of plastic against plastic. "There. The world is a tiny bit better now."

"I'm not arguing with you over the value of those causes. They are definitely worth speaking up about. But do you think shouting at an asshole biker is going to do anything? If he heard you, it would probably only inflame him."

The light changes and we cross, hitting the next block. "I disagree. I bet it'd make him think twice next time," I say, holding my ground.

Her eyebrow climbs, then she laughs and pats my shoulder. "Such an idealist."

My eyes drift to her hand. To those long fingers curled over me momentarily. To the casual every-dayness of her touch. We were like this before—playful touches, friendly hugs, the kind of tangled up in each other that you can only be in college with a big group of friends spread out across futons, listening to music, eating takeout, and debating the future of art, business, and the world itself.

And then, for one brief night, she and I were more.

Now, her eyes lock with mine, and heat flashes in her irises, a look I remember far too well. It pairs perfectly with that scorching memory of her calling out my name. She yanks her hand away, stuffing both into her jeans pockets.

"Anyway, thank you for saving me from the biker," she says. She's suddenly cool Lola again, in-charge Lola, marching forward to the stupidly named button shop.

That's the Lola I know.

Not the one who gabs about silly names and remembers my passions from college.

And definitely not the one whose heart seemed to race too, when she fell into my arms.

Though to be fair, she *was* nearly run over.

Yes, I am an idealist, but I'm also a realist. That's the part of me that knows better than to entertain any dangerous thoughts about Lola.

When we arrive at the button shop a few minutes later, a memory clambers up inside me—the image of my brother dressed as Anakin Skywalker. But it wasn't a button Rowan needed for his costume. He was hunting for an Anakin Skywalker comic book. I shake my head adamantly when I scan the shelves from the window. "This is wrong. This isn't where they met. They met at a comic book shop. I'm sure of it."

She rolls her eyes as she reaches for the handle, jerking her head toward the inside of the store. "No, they didn't. They met *here*. Luna told me all about it. How their eyes locked over a jar of plaid buttons. How he asked what it was for and listened intently as she detailed her beliefs in good-luck outfits. Something he wholeheartedly agreed with."

I shake my head, digging in my heels. "Nope, it was a comic book store. The one three blocks away. He was doing research for his costume. The Skywalker costume."

"He researches his costumes?"

That's my brother and his passions. "He's extremely committed to costume accuracy and always has been. Halloween isn't just a holiday for him. It's a reason to wake up each morning, because every day is one day closer to the next Halloween."

"And I thought I was a Halloween fangirl because I like those Costco mini peanut butter cups you only see in October," she says offhand.

I scoff. "Great. Tempt me with peanut butter cups."

She lifts a brow. "I didn't realize that was your temptation."

"You said it yourself, woman. They're the best peanut butter cups under the sun, and now I'm starving. So, thanks for that."

She pouts sympathetically. "Aww, poor Lucas. Want me to get you some for your craving?"

"Yes. It can be my reward for being right. Because I'm positive they met at the comic shop."

Her eyes are fiery as she stares at me—a hard, you're-so-wrong stare. "And I'm positive they met here. So, I say winner gets treated to dinner and peanut butter cups, because this girl is ready for food." With that, she jerks open the door and advances into the store like she's leading an army.

"I ate already," I call out. It's a lie though. I'm famished.

But she doesn't care about my appetite, because she's a woman on a mission.

So am I—on a mission, that is.

A quest to avoid the temptation of her again.

Trouble is, she looks insanely hot as she strides over to the counter, acoustic guitar acquisition in her crosshairs.

Damn. There is just something about her confidence that turns me on when it shouldn't.

It shouldn't at all.

Except it always fucking did. Her boldness was my Achilles' heel when I first met her, and it's doing a number on me now too.

6

LOLA

The pink-haired woman with the pierced lip raises one finger. "I'll be right with you, sweetie. Let me just finish with Sabrina." She scurries to the corner of the shop, joining a customer who's surveying brass buttons.

"Thanks," I say, a little strained because I want to get this show on the road.

But I have to wait till she's free.

Maybe this will be a chance to scope out the competition for the award. Dig into his approach for his presentation. Except how the hell do I butter him up to tell me a damn thing?

By chatting more.

A simple conversation.

Yes, that'd be the best way.

As the two women talk, I wander past the pink pastel shelves, checking out jars of buttons. "So, here we are," I say, with an impatient sigh. "Exactly where I thought I'd be spending my Friday night."

"Where did you think you'd spend it? Did you have a *hot date* you had to cancel?" Lucas ends the question with a saucy little sound, like he's toying with me.

Time for me to toy with him.

I tap my chin, staring at the ceiling. "Not tonight. Pretty sure the hot date was slated for tomorrow. I wonder what I should wear . . ."

He scoffs. "Is he taking you to the mall? Or a fast-food restaurant?"

I shoot him a withering look. "No. A club. Dancing. I think I'll wear something sexy. Maybe that shows a little midriff," I say, teasing him too, because I know his weakness. His eyes always went a bit glossy when I wore short shirts. I don't even think he was aware of his addiction.

Or . . . that he still has it. Because he licks his lips when I describe the possible outfit. Oh my. Lucas still loves a hint of skin. "How does that sound?" I ask innocently.

His expression is stone-hard. "Don't wear that."

I crease my brow. "No? Are you sure? It sounds like good clubbing attire."

"A sweater is better." His voice is rough now, like he's having trouble getting the words out.

I tap my chin, like I'm deep in thought. "A sweater? That doesn't sound like I can shimmy my hips easily in it." I give a little sway for demonstration. He's like a dog watching a piece of steak. "I think something nice and snug would do the trick on a white . . . hot . . . date."

His jaw ticks. His lips are a ruler. "I hear overalls are hip." It sounds like he drank battery acid.

Oh, I could put him out of his silly jealousy-fueled misery, but I don't want to. And playing the flirt is much more fun than the thought of playing Double-O-Seven.

I smile widely. "Good idea. Overalls can be hot. Maybe I could get some overall shorts and just wear a teeny-tiny sports bra underneath." I turn my attention to a jar of rhinestone-encrusted buttons, grinning privately.

He steps closer, then clears his throat. "So, you do?"

"Do what?"

"Do you have a hot date tomorrow night?"

I peer at him out of the corner of my eye as I dip a hand into the jar, fingering some buttons. "I don't know. I'd have to check my calendar."

"Guess we better finish by tomorrow night, then," he says, like the words are strangling him. "Don't want you to miss a possible date."

Or maybe *he's* strangling the words, because it sounds like he wants to throttle the idea of me having a date. I spin around, meeting his gaze.

Holy shit.

His eyes blaze at me, dark and shimmering with envy. It's unexpectedly arousing. Tingles spread down my arms as gooseflesh rises over my skin. Lucas Xavier is jealous, and it turns me on.

Just like it did years ago.

"Exactly. I wouldn't want to either." I toy with him as

I run my fingers over the buttons, like they're on a man's shirt.

His eyes pin mine. He's like a gunslinger in the Old West, refusing to back down. "I'm sure Mr. Fabulous will take you to a perfectly average club, engage in by-the-book dancing, mix in some standard getting-to-know-you conversation, then walk you home like a perfect gentleman and ask if he can call you the next day. That sounds terrific, doesn't it?"

Sounds like the battery acid is now mixed with arsenic.

I tap my chin, considering such a date, toying with him more. "That doesn't sound too bad. But what if I don't want him to be a perfect gentleman?"

Flames lick over his eyes. Plumes of jealousy rage around him. But he doesn't say anything. He reaches into the jar, fishes around for a button, and brushes his fingers across mine.

I gasp.

A blatantly obvious gasp.

Dammit. I gave myself away.

He grins, the satisfied smirk of a man who knows what he's doing. Right now, he's doing me. Stroking one long finger across the top of my hand. "Then make sure to tell him you'd rather he toss you over his shoulder, carry you up the steps, and show you all the ways he can be ungentlemanly."

My knees go weak. My breath hitches. And my hand defies me, staying there, asking for more of his touch.

More of these taunting little strokes, like he's proving I don't have a date just by touching me.

His talented fingers feel so damn good on mine.

But I have to get a handle on this latent lust. I can't let it control me.

Squaring my shoulders, I remove my hand from the jar. "I'll be sure to give him that message," I say in my best cool voice.

I swivel around, suddenly fascinated with a jar of pink buttons.

"Don't worry. I'm sure he can figure that out on his own," he whispers.

Yes, I suspect Lucas has figured that out too. And his jealousy turns me on too much for my own good, so I choose another tactic.

Honesty.

"I don't have a date," I say, going for directness. "Not tonight, not tomorrow, not for the foreseeable future."

His expression shifts instantly. Gone is the caveman. In its place is a thinking man, asking questions. "You're not seeing anyone?"

I shake my head. "No. Work keeps me busy."

He swallows roughly, nods, then says, "Same here."

It sounds like it costs him something to admit that, and that's why I let my guard down a little more. "I was supposed to have coffee with a client this evening. To go over some of the designs I'm working on for him. But I pushed it to the morning to deal with this."

He wiggles his brows. "Ah, so I did ruin your Friday

night plans. Or wait, maybe this makes me your one night stand-in?"

I laugh. "Yes. That's exactly what you are. My one night stand-in for work. Since that's what I'm usually doing at night. I started my own design firm a few months ago. I went to a contract role at Bailey & Brooks. I'm working insane hours, but I love it," I say, and right now I love this honest moment with him. It reminds me of how we used to talk to each other. When we were friends. When we shared our hopes and dreams.

And those dreams didn't involve *spying* on the competition, so I let that notion go. As much as I want to win the award, I'm not a secret agent. I'm just a woman who loves her sister like crazy. That's why I'm with Lucas tonight—for Luna.

So what if I let myself momentarily enjoy a conversation with the man who was once a confidante and a very kindred spirit?

Especially since he seems to be enjoying himself too, judging by the hint of a smile on his lips. "That's great, Lola. I always imagined you'd do your own thing."

"You did?"

"Yeah, you never seemed like the kind of woman who'd want to take orders. You want to give the orders."

I laugh at his assessment—the truthfulness of it, and the reality, too, of running a business. "Mostly I'm giving orders to myself."

It's his turn to laugh. "Yep. I know that well. Morning, noon, and night. It's a never-ending list of things you need to do."

"But you wouldn't change it?" I ask, curious to know if he's happy too. If the dreams of his twenty-one-year-old heart have come true nearly ten years later.

"Nah. I'm too opinionated to work effectively for someone else."

I let my jaw hang open. "You? Opinionated? I had no idea."

"Pretty shocking, isn't it?" He drums his fingers along the shelf near a jar of silvery buttons. They seem to catch his gaze. "Speaking of opinions, the cover you did for *Sex and Other Shiny Objects*?"

I brace myself at the mention of a romantic comedy that Amy edited. It hit bookstores a month ago. And considering he told me my *Fashion Roadkill* cover looked like it was designed by a pigeon on meth, I'm betting he has nothing nice to say about the silvery buttons on the cover of the rom-com. "Yes, Lucas?"

His eyes meet mine again, and they're softer this time, a little gentler. "Terrific cover. One of your best."

My stupid heart glows. I shouldn't like his praise so much. But I do, oh, how I do. Because he's so damn talented, and because he rarely doles out praise. "Thank you. That one has a special place in my heart."

"As it should," he says.

"And while we're at it, I should tell you that your *If Found, Please Return cover* was fantastic. It wasn't derivative at all. It was great."

"Thank you," he says, a genuine smile playing on his lips.

"It's going to be tough going up against you in the competition." That admission hurts my professional soul the slightest bit, but it's also freeing.

He takes a beat. "I can absolutely say the same about you."

A voice cuts in. "Thank you so much for waiting. What can I do for you?"

The pink-haired woman flashes a happy-to-help grin, and I wish the other customer had taken all night. Because I was actually enjoying that moment of truth with Lucas. It felt like old times, when we spoke to each other from our hearts and souls.

But I have to set that moment aside, because I'm here for one reason, and it's not to tease Lucas, or to glean intel. Nor is it to get to know him all over again.

"We're here because we're looking for a stash of acoustic guitars," I begin, then dive into the story. When I finish, I add, "I know it sounds crazy, and I feel a little crazy asking. But I'm sure my sister and Rowan met here, so I figured this must be where the landlord left the guitars as part of his caper. Any chance you have a couple guitar cases from Harrison Bates?" I ask hopefully. Hell, I practically bat my lashes.

"I wish," she says.

That response doesn't compute. "You wish?"

She sighs in longing. "My God, that sounds like a fantastic way to spend a Friday night. To be enlisted in a scavenger hunt. That's like an awesome Sunday Funday activity, only it's Friday. It's a sign that this is going to be a great weekend."

Enlisted. That's an interesting way of putting it. I imagine Harrison lining up his troops, prepping them for his grand payback adventure.

I try again, hoping to jog her memory, while my pseudo ex leans against the wall like he's waiting, just waiting to say *I told you so.*

That's the reminder I need of who he is. He's not the man who doles out earnest praise. He's the man who wants me to be wrong. The man who didn't apologize.

I snap my gaze to the woman in pink. "And you're positive, Eloise?" I ask, reading her name tag. "My sister has told me about your store. She's obsessed with buttons." I implore her because the guitars *must* be here. "And she bought the—"

"The red-and-gray plaid ones," Eloise chirps. "She showed me her costume when she finished it. She was the most adorable—"

"Schoolgirl," supplies Lucas in a sexy rumble. "She went as a schoolgirl. Like I said, they met at the comic book shop. He was working on his costume. The store is a few blocks away."

My shoulders tighten, and I swear I'm clutching the edge of a windowsill of a tall brick building, clinging white-knuckled, rather than climbing in and admitting I'm wrong. "Fine. Let's go to the comic shop." I turn to Eloise. "Thank you though. You were so helpful."

"Anytime! And if you ever need buttons, I'm your

girl." She waves as we head to the door. "And tell Baxter I said hi."

I stop, swivel around. "Who's Baxter?"

"He runs the comic book store. He's a sweetie pie. Everyone loves him."

"Thanks, Eloise," Lucas says. "I'll say hi to Baxter for you."

After we leave, I brace myself for Lucas to slice, dice, and I-told-you-so me to ribbons. It's coming, and it's going to suck.

7

LOLA

But as we hit the sidewalk, maintaining a rapid clip, he only smiles and waits.

"Fine," I blurt out after two blocks like that, frustration bubbling over in me. "Fine, they met at the comic shop. You're right. You're so right. What do you want on your sandwich?"

"*Everything.*" Each syllable drips with sex and self-satisfaction.

This man has turned into such a cocky bastard.

Except, wait.

Wait a freaking minute.

Something doesn't add up with his comic shop logic. "Hold on," I say, slamming my arm against his chest—his solid-as-a-plank chest. Were his muscles this firm in college? Actually, they were. A college athlete, the man knew how to treat his body like a temple.

"Ouch," he teases, adopting an over-the-top wince.

"Stop it. It didn't hurt. You're built of concrete."

He wiggles a brow. "Thanks. Lacrosse helps."

I grit my teeth. Like I want a reminder of that sport. "Of course you still play."

"It wasn't the sport's fault, Lola."

"I'm well aware of that," I say coolly, then I draw a deep, calming breath. It doesn't matter what happened that weekend in college. Doesn't matter how he ditched me after kissing me passionately—and more—and asking me out.

Doesn't matter that I'd waited in my dorm for our first date, all dressed up, ready to go with him to a department dinner, or that I'd gone alone instead.

When he didn't show up that night or the next, I was so hurt, then so mad, then so certain he'd thought our night together had been a mistake.

I was only twenty-one, fueled by dreams, ambitions, and desires. I wanted it all. I wanted him.

And then I didn't have him.

And it hurt like hell.

When he finally appeared at my door and rattled off the events of that weekend, detail by painstaking detail —*the guys came by, blindfolded us, took us camping; it was fun, but still*—I'd wound myself up too far to simply let down my guard and say, *Hey, it happens. Come on in and kiss me like crazy.*

Besides, I needed him to apologize first, and when he didn't lead with that, my walls went up again, brick by brick.

It was for the best, I told myself.

We were better off as friends.

I wasn't interested in jocks anyway.

I told myself the universe had saved me from giving my heart to someone who didn't deserve it.

If he couldn't lead with *I'm sorry,* couldn't weave that into the opening notes of his *I'm back* song, how could I let him know how much he meant to me?

Friendship was the only way out. The only path that didn't lead to my becoming a fool in love like my mom and dad. I'd seen exactly where that kind of starry-eyed, us-against-the-world mentality led—to them ignoring their own children.

And he'd affirmed my decision when he made that callous comment—*It was just one night anyway.*

Exactly.

That was all it was.

And that's all tonight is. One stupid night to get through.

And I'm here for Luna.

I'm about to tell him why I don't believe Luna went to the comic shop when he continues about lacrosse.

"And yes, I still play," he says. "I joined a league, and we play in Central Park on weekends, and nobody kidnaps me and takes my phone away." There's a note of contrition in that last bit, but it's ten years too late.

"Glad to hear your phone is in your control." I clip my reply and return to the task at hand. "My point is this—Luna is not a comic book fan. She doesn't go to comic shops. She would never have been there on her own. Even if Rowan was doing research for his costume, and even if Luna went to a party as a schoolgirl, that doesn't mean she was in the shop at the same time as he was. We don't know for sure they met there."

"No, we don't. But it's likely. She went to the button shop, then to the comic shop, because even if she's not a fan of comic books, I bet she knows Baxter. He's a fixture around here. She probably went there to say hi to him."

I groan inside. Who the hell is this Baxter guy? "She's friends with Baxter and went there to say hi to him? Doubtful."

"Actually, it's not doubtful at all. It's perfectly logical. You know, *logic*," he says slowly. "That thing that helps rational people make sense of events that have transpired? Like, say, when a guy can't reasonably return in time from a trip?"

Forget burning. I am a volcano. I am about to spew red-hot lava that will eat him alive. "Yes. I am familiar with rational thought. Something I've been practicing for years, like a religion. But, by all means, please illuminate your rationale. Be my guest."

I sweep out my arm and let the jackass take the lead, and as I do, I offer up ten million prayers to all the gods and goddesses, all saying . . .

Let him be wrong.

I don't care where the freaking guitars are right now. I want this man to be wrong more than I want a sandwich, and I am famished.

When we enter the comic shop, the burly man behind the counter welcomes us with a jovial Santa

Clausesque "Heya! Welcome to Baxter's Comic Book Haven."

Lucas heads to the counter. "Hey, Bax. How the hell are you?"

"Good to see you again, my man." They do some guy-type fist bumping. What the hell? Lucas knows Baxter too?

"Been a while," Lucas says. "How's it going? How's Annie? Is she still on the mend?"

The bearded man beams. "She's great. Kicked that stage-two bitch like the badass she is. One full year in remission."

Ohhhhh.

I get it now.

I understand his logic completely.

The comic shop is a real possibility now. Luna loves people. Loves the neighborhood. Luna wouldn't have come in here for comics, but she definitely would have come in to check on this man and his wife. That's my sweetheart of a sister.

Lucas's smile is magnetic. "Awesome. Nothing better than that."

"That's fantastic. So wonderful," I chime in, because the news this man is sharing is the kind that any human would be happy to hear.

"Thank you. Appreciate you saying that." Baxter swings his eyes to Lucas. "And we appreciate you making that donation to research. Means the world to us."

Okay, I am officially living in an alternate world. One where Lucas is kind and thoughtful and giving.

"Least I can do," Lucas says with a deferential nod.

Baxter rubs his palms together. "Now, what can I do for you? Did you decide to finally get into *Superman*? Or did you want to buy the newest *Star Wars* collection for Ro's birthday?"

"Definitely the new *Star Wars*. Why don't you set it aside for him?" Lucas says, then fishes into his wallet and slaps down a credit card. "He will lose his mind with happiness. But I'm also here because I'm hoping you can help us out with something."

"I'm always happy to give you a hand, and you know that, but"—Baxter tips his forehead to me and clears his throat exaggeratedly—"maybe first, you finally want to introduce me to your kind lady friend?"

"Ah, yes. Baxter, this is Lola. Lola, meet Baxter," Lucas says, and I extend a hand.

"Nice to meet you," I say.

"Likewise. And it's about time," Baxter says, his eyes drifting to Lucas. "I've heard so much about you from him."

I flinch. I must be hearing things. Must be the hunger causing aural hallucinations. "All fabulous stuff, I'm sure," I joke, since I'm sure it was nothing of the sort.

"Definitely all good," Baxter says, dead serious.

And I'm thoroughly confused. Lucas appears flummoxed too. Except is that a hint of red coursing over his carved cheeks?

I do believe Lucas is blushing.

I rein in a smile. I shouldn't feel so delighted over this little discovery, yet I do. Because maybe, just maybe, he didn't entirely mean it when he said, *It was only one night.* Maybe I've haunted his dreams since then. I like that possibility, for more reasons than I care to unpack right now.

"Baxter, my man. Let's not let the lady know all my secrets," Lucas says, like he's desperately trying to sweep something under the rug.

Baxter chuckles, then brings a finger to his lips. "Then I won't tell her you thought she looked stunning in all black at that party a year ago. The same one that Rowan worked on the costume for."

A gong clangs.

A bell rings.

And Lucas and I both look at each other. I suspect my expression mirrors his. *Eureka.*

"They went to that party? The same one we went to?" I ask, shock racing through me as I picture the new bowling alley in Chelsea, the retro-style place that's all the rage now. "The one at Pin-Up Lanes?"

Lucas scrubs a hand across his stubbled jaw. "I never saw him there. That's why I didn't think they met at that party. But they must have."

My smile widens. "Definitely. Maybe just for a few seconds. I invited Luna to go with me, but I didn't think she ever showed up. Which is typical for her." I bounce on my heels, ready to hitch a flying carpet to Manhattan to get the damn guitars.

"And I invited Rowan to go with me. But I didn't think he showed up. Which is also typical for him."

"Or maybe you were too busy checking out the cat," Baxter says in a stage whisper. "Oops."

I grin wickedly, like a sexy black cat, because that little nugget makes me purr. Maybe I'm vain, or maybe I'm simply human. But for the longest time, I've been sure that Lucas had never been into me the same way I was into him. That he'd rejected the possibility of *more* with me and his parting comment that weekend was his sole truth.

Perhaps it wasn't.

"It was a good costume," Lucas says, owning it.

"Glad you enjoyed my fierce feline look," I say, a little flirty, and it feels like I've slipped back in time to that night we were tangled up together, kissing deeply, holding tightly.

"It was the fiercest." His voice dips to an appreciative rumble.

Sparks shimmy over my skin, but I ignore them. "And what were you that night? If memory serves, there was shirtlessness involved."

"A fireman," he says, a little smoky.

An image flashes before my eyes. Lucas, in turnouts, suspenders, and no shirt. No wonder I don't remember if my sister was at the party.

But today I'm operating with blinders on, because I'm here for a reason.

For Luna.

The person I love. The person I look out for. She's

my little bird, and she needs help, even if she made this mess.

I turn to Baxter, needing to make sure we're following the right clues. "This means you don't have the guitars? The ones the landlord left?"

Baxter shakes his head. "No guitars here."

We thank Baxter and catch a cab to Pin-Up Lanes. As soon as I click my seat belt in, my phone dings with a text message. The *Charlie's Angels'* theme music tells me it's my group chat with Amy and Peyton.

Amy: Dear Diary, it is nearly nine and we have not heard from Lola. We fear she is trapped in a sexy-ex vortex. We will continue to hold out hope for her.

Lola: There is no vortex, I assure you.

Peyton: She's alive! But how do we know this is truly you? Prove it. What does Lola have tattooed on her ass?

Amy: Wait. Lucas might know that. Ask something else.

Peyton: You're right. The confidentiality of ass tattoos is too easily compromised. How about this? What did Lola recommend I keep an open mind about when I was in the midst of the Project Sexy Scenes research last fall with Tristan?

Lola: Lube! Also, I do not have an ass tattoo. Or any tattoos for that matter!

Peyton: You passed!

Amy: It's you! You're safe! Hallelujah!

Lola: Yes, you devils. It's me. I'm fine, and everything is fine, and we are making progress.

Amy: Define "progress." Are you: A) Fighting with him? B) Rolling your eyes at him? C) Wondering what he looks like naked?

Lola: All of the above, but I'm not acting on C. We're going to Pin-Up Lanes for guitars.

Peyton: Get the rosemary fries there. They are delish.

Lola: I know! I don't ever resist rosemary fries from Pin-Up Lanes.

Amy: Words to live by. But before the great French fry consumption begins, what is the status of your efforts to tango horizontally with the one who got away?

Lola: I never said he was the one who got away.

Amy: You don't have to. That's what we call him on your behalf. When we aren't hating him for you.

Peyton: Do you need a sexy new bra-and-panty set first? Because I can messenger one from my store to your place stat.

Lola: No bra-and-panty set is necessary for fry-eating because there will be no removal of clothes. We are on our way to a freaking bowling alley.

Amy: You're going to get naked with him there? Like, at the ball return? In the restroom? Or will you do it on the scoring table? Also, does this mean the hating is over?

Peyton: Nudity at a bowling alley ought to make for an interesting Friday night.

Before I can tap out another response, we pass a cheese shop.

"Stop!" Lucas shouts.

The cab squeals to the curb.

"What the hell?" I ask.

"The Star Wars shirts," he says, a smile lighting up his face. "The note said: *Because your Star Wars T-shirts are where you argued over where you first met! Hint: there was cheese involved, you little hipsters.*"

And my expression matches his. "Yes! She loves going there."

The sign on *The Grater Good* says it closes at eight, so

we rush in with three minutes to spare. This feels like how we were. This was us back in college before everything went belly-up—having fun, playing games, exploring the city together.

Lucas marches over to the bearded man in a leather apron who's arranging handwritten signs in front of the cheese display. "Friday night cheese craving? I can solve that," the man says with a smile.

"Excellent. I'll take some Gouda and whatever the lady wants if you tell me you've got a bag of Star Wars T-shirts with our name on them?"

The man smiles. "As a matter of fact, I do."

And we leave a minute later, with Star Wars T-shirts, a wedge of Gouda for him, and some Manchego for me.

And cheesy grins on our faces too.

Two down. Five to go.

The guy with the vest and horn-rimmed glasses lugs two guitars out from behind the counter at the bowling alley, and I clap my hands with excitement. Progress rocks.

"Thank you so much," I tell him.

"No problem. But I'm not gonna lie. I didn't think you'd make it tonight," the guy says, shaking his head. "Even had a bet going with Harrison when he dropped these off."

I furrow my brow. "You did?"

"Hell yeah. We played a round, he bowled three

hundred, then asked me to store these things. And I said if you weren't here by the end of tonight, he'd owe me a six-pack." The man smiles ruefully. "Kinda wish you'd shown up later."

Lucas laughs. "I'll send you a six-pack myself as a thanks for keeping these safe"—Lucas scans the name tag on the man's tweed vest—"Parker."

Parker's gray eyes light up. "Yeah? You would?"

"Sure. You kept these safe for my brother. What's your poison and when does your shift end?"

Parker says midnight and names his favorite IPA while Lucas taps his phone. He swipes a few more times. "Done. Delivery for you coming at midnight. Thanks again."

"That's awesome." Parker gives him a thumbs-up. "Rock on."

"Same to you," Lucas says, and it's funny that a self-proclaimed "yeller at people" is actually so good with people when he needs to be.

"Thanks, Parker," I call out as the man returns to the counter to check in a new group of bowlers. Then to Lucas, I say, "Amazing how happy a few beers can make a guy."

"Beer—the universal man currency," Lucas says.

"Chocolate—the universal woman currency."

"I'll have to remember that."

"Yes, please store that safely away." I point to a free table in the restaurant section of the alley. "Sandwich?"

Lucas smiles. "I'm starving."

I nudge him with my elbow. "And I thought you said

you weren't hungry."

"Guess I worked up an appetite," he says wryly. "Also, it's my treat."

"You don't have to pay. We can go dutch."

"C'mon, Dumont. You were the first to say *'Pin-Up Lanes.'*"

"But you figured out the cheese shop," I point out, smiling inside because we're *mostly* getting along. That will make it easier to make it through the long night. All we have to do is focus on the present, because rehashing the past makes me see red.

"But the bet was for the first clue," he adds. "Ergo, the meal is on me."

I hold up my hands in surrender. "My stomach won't let me turn you down." We head to the table, and he angles the two guitar cases against the wall. I nod at the instruments. "I live a few blocks away. We can drop those off after this so we don't have to lug them around all night."

"Good plan," he says, then opens the menu on the table, closing it one second later. "Burger for me."

"And a portabella mushroom sandwich for me," I say, remembering fondly all our meals together in school, and how when we got along, we were a freaking house on fire. "They're the best. Especially with the rosemary fries."

He groans. "Damn. Just tempt me a little more."

"Fries were always your weakness," I say. "Even the cafeteria ones."

"And do you blame me? Those were insanely good. I

think they seasoned them with some intoxicating drug designed to make you eat them every night."

"I believe it's called salt and carbs."

"Ah, yes. That's definitely a designer drug, and I'm addicted to it."

"I'd sell my soul for those rosemary fries though. They're that good."

"Let's make it a double, then."

A waiter swings by, and we place our orders, adding a beer for Lucas and a gin and tonic for me.

When the waiter leaves, Lucas stares at me, an intense look in his dark eyes. It's a look I remember from when we used to go to museums together and check out the art, studying it from different angles, trying to find hidden meanings in it. Back when we were friends.

I furrow my brow. "Is everything okay?"

"I was just thinking about tonight. It's kind of funny that they argue about where they met. Whether it was the party or the button shop or the comic shop. I think maybe they saw each other at those other places, but they didn't"—he stops to sketch air quotes—"*officially meet* till the party."

"That makes sense with Luna's version of the locked eyes across the button shop."

"And neither one of us figured out the correct answer to the first clue because we were both too distracted at the party to notice they'd even been there for a few minutes."

"Speak for yourself. I wasn't distracted," I say,

goading him because I can.

His gaze locks with mine. "I *was* speaking for myself. I was definitely distracted by you at that party," he says, and my skin sizzles as he does that thing again with his voice, letting it dip low and sexy. "But hey, if you don't want to admit you were distracted, that's fine. I'll keep your secret, Dumont."

I groan. "You're infuriating."

"So are you. Especially since you refuse to admit how sidetracked you were by my fireman costume, when I've already opened my heart and told you how I felt about your pussycat."

"Oh my God, that's hardly opening your heart," I say, laughing.

He smiles. "Maybe it is though."

"Okay. Your big fireman's heart was *so* distracting," I tease.

"Thank you," he says, straightening his shoulders. "I had a feeling it was. What with my heart being covered in concrete and all." He pats his pecs. "Your words, darling."

I roll my eyes. "Like I said, you're infuriating."

"And I'll take it as a compliment, since you're exactly the same way," he says, but then he drops the teasing like it's a hot poker. He leans forward and scrubs a hand across his chin, like he's deep in thought. "But here's the other thing that's funny. We kind of argued over the same thing way back when. How we met. Do you remember?"

You bet I do.

8

LUCAS

I can still picture the day perfectly. I can recall how we chatted during our graphic design studio class junior year and finally exchanged names.

"It was Professor Trumbull's Wednesday afternoon studio design class," I say, picturing Lola in her jeans and pink T-shirt with a sparkled skull design on the front, extending a hand. "We were paired up on a project, and that's when I introduced myself."

"Yes, and you said, *I'm Lucas Xavier from São Paulo.*" She gestures for me to speed the story along.

I tap my temple. "And I thought to myself, if she's half as interesting as she is pretty, then I am going to be so fucked for the rest of the semester."

She furrows her brow like my answer doesn't compute. "That's what you thought?"

I lean closer. "I make no bones about it. I'm a designer, like you, and it's both my passion and my job to look for beauty. You were and are beautiful. I saw it in you then and was drawn to it." I say it matter-of-factly because it's the truth.

I've never *not* been attracted to her. I just didn't act on it for a long time because we were friends. Because I valued that friendship deeply. But that kind of intel stays in the vault.

These details though? It's hard to keep them locked up tonight, especially after Baxter kicked that door open. But what's the harm in her knowing I think she's stunning?

No harm, no foul.

She parts her lips but doesn't seem to know what to say. Which is rare for Lola. Soon enough, though, she finds her voice. "Thank you for that interesting answer."

"Why is it interesting?"

"Because it's deeper than saying, *Hey man, she's a babe*," she says in a bro voice.

"You're also a babe. A smoke show. A total fucking fox," I say, lest she think I'm simply an art aficionado, when I'm definitely still a red-blooded man. "But stop distracting me again. Point being, that's when we met—in class—but you argued with me incessantly over that point."

She slams her palm against her forehead. "Oh my God, Lucas! We didn't meet in that class. We met at the freaking museum. We were both looking at a Jackson Pollock, and we had a long and detailed conversation about whether abstract art could truly represent a real thing." She crosses her arms in conversational victory. "Don't try to deny it. We talked about Pollock's work and the other expressionists and the whole idea of representation. And later we discussed it constantly over study sessions, over lunch in the cafeteria, over coffee, and so on."

I hold up a finger to make a point, enjoying this trek down memory lane. "I remember meeting you at our favorite café, ordering a black coffee for you, with one packet of sugar. And I vividly recall those torturous study sessions when we had to prep for the brutal exams in our business principles class."

"I had to poke you to keep you awake in the lounge as we studied," she says, stretching across the table and stabbing her unpolished fingernail against my arm. The lack of polish shouldn't affect me one way or the other, but I've always liked that Lola's a low-maintenance kind of gal. She doesn't doll herself up to an unrecognizable degree.

"I still have the flesh wounds from your efforts."

"You have the passing grade from my efforts, mister. I saved your ass in business principles, Lucas Xavier," she says, narrowing her eyes, though her tone is full of jest, full of friendship. Like she was before that weekend. Before I fucked things up. Before I said things I shouldn't have and didn't say the things I should.

If I'd been more honest with her the weekend I went away, things might have been different. But when you spend a weekend with a bunch of college guys, you aren't always thinking straight about how to communicate all the crazy feelings you have for a woman.

And at twenty-one, I hardly knew what to say.

Honest affection, open communication—those weren't classes my parents taught. Hiding, avoiding, denying—that was what I grew up seeing.

That had been familiar, and I'm not sure I'm much better at communication now.

But at least one thing is different nearly ten years later. Even though we're arguing, we're having fun as we do it.

And hell, do I ever miss this.

This is what I've missed most since our friendship did a Humpty Dumpty all that time ago. There was no putting it back together again, so we splintered into enemy factions, weapons always drawn.

Tonight though? We're friends again. It's a one night stand-in, and I'll take it.

"Fine, you saved my sorry ass," I concede. "But my point, woman, is this." I slap a hand on the table for emphasis. "We met in class, but you insisted on arguing about whether we actually met at the museum. It was this long, ongoing thing."

"Because we met at the museum," she says, laughing. "You yourself acknowledged we met there."

I shake my head, digging in like the stubborn bastard I am. "Nope. We never exchanged names at the Pollock. Therefore, it was not an official meeting."

She tosses her hands in the air. "See? You are exasperating. Why does it need to be official? We talked for ten minutes before your lacrosse buddy—the guy with red hair, Jimmy or whoever he was—rolled his eyes and pulled you away with an *art is boring* line or whatever."

"Jimmy was the boring one. Which explains why I never stayed in touch with him. Anyway, Boring Jimmy pulled me aside before we exchanged names, which means that you and I didn't officially meet till the graphic design class."

She shakes her head, but she's clearly amused. "It's a wonder we were ever friends at all."

What I wonder more about is what would have happened if we hadn't fallen out of friendship.

But that's the past, and it ought to stay where it is, since my present is just fine, thank you very much.

"Fine, we'll agree to disagree over our first meeting. Just like we did back then," I say with a smile as the waiter brings our drinks. We thank him, and then I clink my glass to hers, the sound drowned out by a ball toppling all ten pins somewhere nearby. When it quiets, I say, "To agreeing to disagree."

"I'll drink to that. Besides, I suspect if Harrison heard us arguing over where we met, he'd throw out our stuff too."

"He'd definitely have grounds to," I say, chuckling. "For a split second this morning, I did wonder whether this was all some big practical joke staged by Rowan."

Her brow creases. "Like a setup for some reason? Or a prank?"

"Yes. But that thought lasted all of ten seconds. He's not a prankster."

"I thought the same thing for about the same amount of time. But Luna's not like that either. It's too much work."

"Agreed. Rowan would never play that sort of joke, and if he was trying to get us to talk to each other . . ."

I trail off. Because if Rowan wanted me to reconnect with Lola for some reason, he'd just tell me to. He saves his energy for songwriting, Luna, and his volunteer work. Not for games. At least, not beyond Monopoly. I swing the conversation in another direction. "I wonder . . . if Harrison had thrown out *our* stuff—would Luna and Rowan have gone hunting for our things?"

Lola smiles, and it's a knowing kind of grin. "Ah, that raises another question, though, doesn't it?"

I know what she's getting at. "Why do we both look after our brother and sister like they're our kids?"

She taps her nose. "Yes, that one indeed."

Because for all the bonding we did over the misery of our required business classes, for all our wonderfully meandering conversations about the meaning of art, the thing that connected us most was our shared background.

Or rather, the sense of responsibility we each came away with.

Different reasons. Same result. We look out for our younger siblings.

I take another drink of the beer, then set it down. "I guess some things never change, do they?"

Sighing, she shakes her head. "I wish they did, but I don't know if they will. I don't know how *not* to look out for Luna," she says, and there are no barbs in her voice now. She doesn't have to add the details I already know well.

When she was sixteen and Luna was twelve, her parents separated, headed straight for a split. But then they decided to go to therapy, and somehow they worked through their troubles. Except once they got back together, they became laissez-faire parents, ignoring their kids.

"You know what happened," Lola continues. "My parents were all about themselves as a couple. Like, they could justify ignoring Luna because they needed to *reconnect* or *have another mommy-daddy vacation*. I didn't want to do that. I wanted to be the one who was there for her, since they weren't."

"I know exactly what you mean." I get it completely. I get *her*. My parents moved here from Brazil when I was five because my father landed a finance job in New York. He became a workaholic, and so did my mom. That drove them apart, splintering their marriage. And they didn't stop. They both worked so damn much post divorce they didn't have time for their kids. I was older and handled it better. But Rowan was always the more sensitive one, more needy. His heart was easily wounded. He was younger too, still moldable clay. And I couldn't stand by and watch them ignore him with their work obsessions, so I became a de facto parent to him. "I hated that they didn't have time for him, and I wasn't going to do the same thing."

"That's why I chose the school I did," Lola confesses quietly. "I don't regret it. I'm glad I went to school where I did. But I did it partly to stay close to her."

"I did the same for him," I admit, something I never

voiced at the time. But I chose a close college so I could keep an eye on him, since the people who were supposed to never did. They were too caught up in work, too intent on lashing out at each other, even after they split.

"Do you ever feel like you love him more than he gives you any reason to?" she asks.

I laugh, but it's tinged with a little sadness as I nod an emphatic yes. "Yeah, I do, but he's like Puss in Boots when he bats his eyes."

"No one can resist those *help me* eyes."

"I'm powerless against him," I admit. "But I don't regret it. He needs someone, and in his own way, he appreciates it. He's grateful, and that seems to hook me every time."

"Luna's the same. Even though she's so needy, she's also so loving. She's like a puppy." Lola sighs, her gaze drifting away. When she speaks again, her voice is low and vulnerable. "Is it our fault that Luna and Rowan are still so dependent at times?"

"That's what my friend Reid says," I admit, flashing back to my conversation with him this morning. "He said I need to learn to say no to Rowan. That I need to let him fend for himself. He's probably right, but it's hard." I can say to Lola what I can't to Reid. He hasn't been through the same things. He hasn't seen a younger sibling start to spiral, to lose their sense of self, and been the only one who tries to help. "I love my kid brother. Flaws and all. Fuckups and all. And I've been saving him since we were kids."

Lola lifts her glass, takes a drink, and exhales. "And I don't know what I'd truly accomplish if I said no to Luna's crazy requests. She's independent; she supports herself. I'm not paying her bills or anything. She's just sometimes a little . . . overly needy."

"And he's sometimes wildly un-independent when it comes to little things," I say.

"So maybe we agree on this point," Lola says, a quirk to her lips.

A grin tugs at mine too. "That there's nothing wrong with helping a sibling?"

She tips her glass to mine. "To family. To loving them, flaws and all."

"I will definitely drink to that." As the crash of pins echoes in the background, I knock back some of the beer, and for the first time in a long time, I feel understood when it comes to my choices about my brother.

I still don't know if I'm doing right by helping him out of every jam. But at least I'm not alone in having no damn clue what the answer is.

The waiter arrives with our food.

"And here are your fries, your sandwich, and your burger. Enjoy," he says.

I grab a fry, and my taste buds cartwheel. "Salt and carbs. My favorite drugs," I say with a happy food moan.

"Mine too," she says, her pretty brown eyes twinkling.

And as I look at her face, I see something so very real —I can still make her smile.

Something I did before.

Something I failed to do when I returned to school.

When I said that shitty thing—*It was only one night.*

I shouldn't have said that.

I should have said a lot of other things.

Talking about my brother reminds me of that. I've had to be the adult with him. I had to take care of him when my parents stopped doing it.

I have no regrets. I love that kid like crazy. I want to give him everything I saw them take away.

But even though I've chosen to play the role of the *mature one* with Rowan, I haven't always done it for myself.

I certainly haven't always done it with the woman across from me.

The night I went to her dorm, I wasn't ready to face the truth of my feelings.

There's no need to now either.

But I can do something I failed to do then.

Maybe it's because of the salt and carb high, or maybe it's because of this crazy night, or possibly it's because not many have the opportunity to say what they should have said way back when . . . Whatever the reason, I draw a deep breath and speak from the heart as she reaches for a fry. "Hey, you."

She looks up in surprise.

The fry falls into the basket as I say, "I'm sorry, Lola."

9

LOLA

They're words I longed to hear nearly ten years ago.

They're the only words I wanted then.

Well, those, followed by *Let's try this whole first date thing again.*

But I can't quite believe he's saying them. And I don't want to misread him. Is he sorry for what happened to us? For our crazy siblings? For our absentee parents?

Or maybe just for the fry that fell?

Nerves thrum through my bones as I wipe my hand on my napkin. "For what, Lucas?"

He heaves a sigh, then rubs a hand across the back of his neck. "There were a lot of things I didn't handle well the night I came to your dorm."

My heart speeds up. It's pumping with anticipation. But not for romance, or for sex. It's an anticipation I didn't expect to feel.

It's the wish for resolution.

To truly put the past behind us.

To say the things we couldn't say as two hotheaded twenty-one-year-old aspiring artists who wanted each other. Who wanted to see if maybe there was something more to all those nights of friendship.

"What sort of things?" I ask, my pitch climbing as I study his handsome features.

Gone is the sexy smirk he wears so well. In its place are serious eyes, flecked with honesty. "For starters, I shouldn't have said that thing about it being only one night. The night before," he explains. "That was dumb and—"

I know exactly what *one night* he means, and I am bursting to say something too, something I didn't even realize I needed to say until just now.

"I'm sorry too," I blurt out, cutting him off, because it feels so damn good to say it at last.

He flinches in surprise. "What are you sorry for?"

And I know. I know exactly what I'm sorry for. I didn't give him a chance to truly apologize. Sure, he should have batted first back then. Definitely, he'd needed to explain better. But I was so wounded that I put on my armor immediately. "I didn't give you a real chance to explain. I went into self-protection mode," I say, my voice marked with potholes as we revisit the past.

In the scheme of things, it's not such a terrible moment. No one died, no one fell ill, and no one lost a home.

But even if it wasn't *the end of the world*, it was the

end of something else—it marked the end of a fantastic friendship.

There was a before and there was an after. And Lucas and I were never the same.

"Lucas," I say, leaning closer, emotions bubbling up inside me, spilling out. "I was so upset that weekend. When you didn't show. I was . . ." I pause, searching for the right word, recalling how I felt as I waited for the guy who'd rocked my world a few nights before. "Devastated. I was devastated."

His face falls, and sadness clouds his features. "I'm sorry, Lo. I felt like shit. For what it's worth, and I know it's not worth much now, but you were pretty much all I thought about while I was away."

A smile pulls at my lips. "Yeah?"

He nods decisively. "And I was so damn frustrated that I didn't have a way to get in touch with you. And the guys, well, you know how they were. Jock pride and all. The captains basically said, '*If anyone needs to call his mommy or daddy, do it now and do it on speakerphone.*' So yeah, I couldn't." He heaves a sigh, long and full of regret. "In retrospect, I should have. But in retrospect, I should have come to your dorm when the weekend was over and groveled. Got down on my knees and said, 'I'm sorry, can we have a do-over? Here are flowers and chocolate and a thousand mea culpas.'"

My throat tightens with a knot of emotion I barely realized was there. When I part my lips to speak, it loosens. "I would have happily given you a do-over, Lucas," I say, voice wobbly.

The corner of his lips quirks up. "You would have?"

I shrug in admission. No need to lie now. Do I need to tell him I was falling for him? Hell no. That stays under lock and key. But letting him know I was interested back then? That I'd have taken him up on a mulligan? Hell yeah. "I would have. I thought about you that weekend too. But by the time Monday rolled around, all I could say was *Let's just be friends.* It was easier that way. Do you know what I mean?"

He lifts his beer, takes a drink, and nods thoughtfully. "I do, Lola. I do. And that's what I'm most sorry for—that we couldn't fucking figure out how to do that."

I breathe out a sigh. Strange that I'd feel relief. But I do. The loss of what we'd had was a huge weight on my conscience, and it's lifting for the first time as we open up about how flawed we were then, how ill-equipped to navigate the waters of friendship to lust and back with no road map. "I didn't know how either. I suppose I can blame my parents for that," I say dryly.

"Parents are always to blame."

"And truthfully, I *didn't* know how. Didn't have a clue. My parents went from madly in love, to fighting and nearly divorcing, to back together and disgustingly in love, obsessed with each other, ignoring their kids. I was like, *Um, how am I supposed to behave with this guy whose hand was down my pants? Where is the guidebook for that?*"

Lucas smacks the table and laughs so deeply, so loudly that the couple at the table nearest us shoots him the side-eye. But then in the distance someone knocks down several pins, and all is forgiven.

When Lucas recovers, still breathing heavily, he says at a lower volume, "That definitely wasn't in any talk anyone gave me either. *Here, son. This is what you do when a girl you're totally hot for says, 'Let's just be friends.'*"

And I beam. It's vanity—so much vanity—but happiness too. There was a part of me that thought he was turned off by me. Knowing he was turned on makes me feel surprisingly good.

But what feels even better is this honest moment. The admission. The confession.

And most of all, the opportunity this strange night has given us to let go of the ways we hurt each other when we were young and foolish.

Now, I'm nearly a decade older, and I hope a lot wiser.

So I say, "Why don't we try again? To be friends? But mean it this time."

The smile that ignites his face is magical. He extends a hand across the table. "Hi, I'm Lucas Xavier from *São Paulo*. I'd very much like to be your friend."

"I'm Lola Dumont from Miami. And I'd like to be your friend too."

We shake . . . for longer than friends usually shake.

And that, too, feels surprisingly good.

When he lets go of my hand, he gestures to the food. "And, as friends, I say we need to polish off this double serving of fries, play a quick game, then get the show on the road."

"That sounds like an excellent plan."

We eat and talk and laugh, and we don't insult each other. We don't shoot mad glances each other's way.

We simply get along like old times.

Like we did before the night we kissed.

It's as if we've rewound the clock.

But it's even better.

Because we're not twenty-one anymore. We're thirty, and we can make it work this time around.

It's wonderful.

* * *

The bowl of fries is empty. Lucas stares at it like a dog praying more kibble will magically appear in his food dish.

"Aww." I push it an inch or so toward him, an offering. "Do you want to lick it?" I glance around the noisy lounge. "I won't tell a soul."

"Cover me, Dumont. I'm going in." He grabs the bowl, brings it to his face, and pretends to lick.

As he places it back on the table, I laugh, saying, "I told you these were soul-selling worthy."

"You did not lie. This is the number-three item I'd sell mine for."

"That was just a cheap way to get me to ask what items one and two are. Fess up. Now."

He wiggles his brows. "I thought you'd never ask. Of course, saving the forests, the trees, the earth would be number one."

I smile. "That's the Lucas I know. Saving the world."

He parks his hands behind his head. "I'm magnanimous with my soul. I'd totally sell it for Mother Earth's benefit."

"So thoughtful. But, not to knock you down too many pegs, how much do you actually think your soul is worth?" I posit. "How do you know the devil would accept that deal?"

He clasps his hand to his heart, affronted. "I have an excellent soul, thank you very much. I'd like to think it'd command top dollar from Lucifer."

"In that case, I'll schedule the seance to summon the dark lord and get the paperwork ready. What's the second thing?"

He slashes a hand through the air, like he's ridding the planet of another offense. "Erasing all coffee shop phone calls from existence."

"Again, look at you. So considerate. Sacrificing yourself so others won't be aurally accosted in coffee shops."

He shrugs, like it's no big deal. "I'm a generous guy, Lola. I'm looking out for the eardrums of others. Or maybe I just can't take another second of *Can I start my dating profile with 'Is that a turtle in your pocket?'* Or *Dude, I'm so drunk today, but no one at the office could tell. Isn't that rad?* To which I wanted to say, *Everyone could tell.* But wait—there's more! From coffee shop phone calls, I've learned how to fix an old record player, how to trick a guy into thinking he meant to text you, how to convince a woman to dump you first, how to ghost effectively and still look like a nice guy, and where to buy a wet suit in Manhattan."

"And you've been keeping all this from me? Didn't you know I was looking for a wet suit?"

He raises his brows. "Go to Don's Surf Shop on East Fifty-Ninth Street. He'll give you a twenty percent discount if you whisper, '*Fins up.*'"

"I'm so there." I laugh. "Also, is that what people are talking about in cafés? Because if they are, you could write a book—*Things Overheard in Coffee Shops.*" I'm thinking of Amy and her penchant for sniffing out ideas for quirky gift books.

"Caffeine reveals our true selves. And coffee shops are a window into the soul. So, for that book, I'd design a cover featuring latte foam art in the style of Edvard Munch's *The Scream.*"

I can picture it perfectly, and it's so him. "That's a good concept. But here's mine: a coffee cup with head-phones on it."

He strokes his chin, considering. "Yours might be more inviting. Mine could perhaps suggest postapoca-lyptic coffee wars, and that *might* be off-putting."

"Just a tad. And if we go with my concept, we'd make sure the foam art had a wicked grin. Sort of a cheeky nod to either the clandestine joy found in eavesdrop-ping or the satisfaction derived from blocking out the conversations of others."

"That's it. It's official. We're designing it together."

I laugh. "We'll submit it for next year's Design-Off International."

"Speaking of that competition," he says, wiggling his fingers, goading me on, "you know you're dying to tell me about your presentation."

I roll my eyes as I lift my empty glass. "One more gin and tonic, and I'll dish it all up."

He raises a hand and calls *"Oh, waiter"* in jest.

But I don't laugh, because a smidge of guilt settles into my gut. Guilt over my original plan for the evening. And since we're on a truth bender, I follow that path. "I have a confession."

He leans forward and hums invitingly. "I'll be your priest. Tell me your sins."

I draw a breath. "I maybe, possibly, might have been hoping to spy on you tonight." I flash a toothy *please forgive me* grin.

One eyebrow arches. "Is that so? Were you hoping to know what color boxers I'm wearing? Because you can just ask." He whispers, "They're black."

Great. Now I'm thinking about Lucas nearly naked, and it's a mouthwatering image. "That's not my confession." I square my shoulders and press on. "I was actually toying with trying to get some intel on your presentation." It sounds gross as it comes out, but I'm still glad I've said it.

His other eyebrow rises, and he wags a finger at me. "You are nefarious. I mean that as the highest compliment. But I have to ask—how's espionage working out for you?"

I slump. "Turns out I'm a terrible spy. I realized about ten minutes into our night that I wasn't going to be able to extract anything, and I'd also feel like a complete ass if I did. So, there you go. You get two confessions for the price of one."

He leans across the table, sets a hand on my head. "Go in peace, my child." Then his fingers travel a few inches down my hair, sending a traitorous sizzle across my scalp and along my neck. "Also, I'll tell you all about it. Just come a little closer." He pauses, tugs me toward him, licks his lips. *Those lips.* "My presentation is going to be . . . spectacular."

He lets go, and I roll my eyes. "You ass."

"You spy."

"I admitted I spied!"

"I admitted I'm awesome."

"Exasperating. You are still Lucas Exasperating Xavier."

"And you are still as fiery as ever. And just as competitive. It's insanely sexy, so watch out, Dumont. The more you try to spy on me, the more it might turn me on."

A grin takes over my face.

A wicked, naughty grin.

"Now let's see how competitive you are on the lanes," he says.

We play a quick round, and when I beat him, I can't help but wonder if that turns him on too.

* * *

He pays for the game and dinner, then grabs the bag of

clothes and the guitars and nods to the door. "After you."

"Let me carry something," I say when we're on the street.

"Nah, I'm playing a gentleman tonight." Then he goes quiet for a few seconds. Maybe more. "Unless you don't want me to be a gentleman?"

Sparks shoot up my spine, lighting me up, making me hot.

Is that what I want?

Or do I want this renewed friendship?

I want both. That's the trouble. But how can I have both?

Especially when there's something else I need more.

As I cast my eyes on the guitars, the reminder of tonight's mission hits me square in the solar plexus. We have three more to-do-list items to complete, and less than forty-eight hours to do so. It's already ten p.m.

"That is an excellent question," I say, dodging the implications for now as I return to Harrison's jump-through-hoops email. "But another important question is the debate Rowan and Luna had." I recite from the email. *"Remember that debate over who was better at leading and who was better at following? You had it the night you took a certain class. You'll find your iPad there."*

"Ah, yes. The mission." The words are tinged with disappointment, but it's gone quickly, and then he's upbeat again as he looks at his watch. "Let's hope Harrison left it someplace that's still open. We can knock out a third one tonight, and I suspect from that clue that they took a dance class."

My smile brightens. "Yes! That's what I was going to say too. Ballroom dance. Leading and following."

"Because *of course* they'd argue over who was better at that," he says as we cross the street, reaching my block.

"Such an important debate to have." I cycle through my memory bank, trying to recall if Luna mentioned a dance class. "Salsa? Rhumba? Cha-cha? Fox-trot?" I laugh as I remember Peyton's teasing texts from earlier. "Maybe it was the tango."

Lucas is silent for a moment. "Actually, that may be it. Rowan always wanted to learn to tango."

I snap my fingers, wheel toward him, and clasp a hand on his shoulder. "Yes! You're right. I had tango on my mind because of something Peyton said. But Luna mentioned it before too. She said something about getting a red tango dress. They must have taken tango lessons. But who the hell knows where?"

He looks at my hand, his voice low and raspy when he says, "Exactly. There are a ton of dance studios in this city."

I sigh, frustration coursing through me. "Let me try to get an answer from her." I grab my phone and send a text to my sister, asking where she took tango. But I know she won't answer. That stupid boat and its stupid lack of cell service.

I shove the phone back in my pocket. "You can take ballroom dancing anywhere. Hotels have classes.

Broadway rehearsal studios have classes. Freaking nightclubs have classes."

"I can try Rowan. I'll send him a text when we get to your place, but I doubt he'll reply. I haven't heard a word from him all day, and I sent a few messages right after I read the original email this morning. No reply."

I grit my teeth but push my annoyance aside. "We'll figure it out," I say, keeping positive. "We figured out Pin-Up Lanes and the cheese shop. We will figure out the tango place. And I'll shoot Harrison an email to let him know we're on track to meet his deadline."

"I'm sure he'll be thrilled to hear it. Seems like such a delightful guy." Lucas flashes a crooked grin. "But we're kind of brilliant, if you think about it. We can definitely crack the code on . . . tango lessons." Those last two words roll off his tongue with a Latin flavor. He came to the US so young that he never speaks with an accent. But he can slip into a Brazilian one when he needs to, and the sound thrums through me, igniting another wave of sparks.

"Tango sounds hot," I offer.

His lips twitch into a sexy smirk. "Very hot."

I let go of his shoulder, and we resume our pace. My apartment is one hundred feet away.

Fifty.

Twenty-five.

And I ask myself again what I want.

To look up tango clubs?

Or do I want to tango with this man?

Both. All. I want it all. I want this chemistry, and I want the chance at friendship too.

But first, *this.*

When I reach my apartment, I turn to him. "I have the answer to your earlier question."

"I'm all ears," he says, knowing exactly which one I mean.

I'm not sure where this night is going. But I know where *we're* going right now.

Inside.

"The answer is—it depends how ungentlemanly you can be," I say, leaving a brand-new opportunity wide open.

"I can be incredibly ungentlemanly," he says.

When the door falls shut behind us, I find out exactly how much.

10

LUCAS

Friendship is awesome.

Letting go of the past is great.

Helping my brother is in my DNA.

But kissing Lola? Yeah, I'd sell half my soul for that.

Only, I don't need to. I don't need to text my brother either. Because this landlord quest is the last thing on my mind right now.

The second the door closes to her apartment, I set down the guitars and bags, back her up to the wall, and run my fingers down her bare arm. Gooseflesh rises on her skin. Her breath hitches. She flicks on a light. And she arches toward me.

Yes.

I'd like a little something just for me right now.

Not for work. Not for family. And not for any other reason than the simplest.

Want.

I wanted her a decade ago. I want her even more now.

I lift my hand and run my thumb along her jaw. "Just so you know, if I took you on a date tonight, I'd take you out to dinner. I'd walk you home. But I'd also definitely fuck you."

Her eyes widen invitingly, and her hand darts out, grabbing my belt, yanking me toward her. "How do you know I'd let you?"

I wiggle a brow. "I can be very convincing."

"Convince me." Her fingers play with the waistband of my jeans.

"Let's see if this convinces you." I brush my thumb over her bottom lip, and she shivers. Inching closer, I whisper, "I still remember how your lips taste."

"How do they taste?"

"Incredible," I say, as a rumble works its way up my chest. "So fucking incredible. But I keep wondering . . ."

I let my other hand travel down her side, along the edge of her breast to her waist. Her sexy stomach. My God, I could not keep my eyes off her whenever she showed a sliver of this fantastic stomach. I wrap my hand around her trim body, as she asks, "What are you wondering?"

I don't tell her the whole truth. That I've thought about her over the years, remembered our kiss with both desire and regret. That I've wondered what would have happened between us—not only on our first date, but after that.

Now isn't the time to share those truths, so I stick to

a simpler one. "I was wondering how much better you'd taste tonight. Especially since I've been wanting to kiss these lips since I first saw you outside my brother's place."

"Don't wait," she says.

"I won't." I seal my lips to hers, groaning the second we make contact. Sweet and fiery. That's how she tastes.

I slide my hand along her jaw, cupping her cheek, holding her gorgeous face.

Taking my time, I kiss her slowly, teasing her, taunting her.

Wanting to hear her gasp, to feel her squirm against me.

And she does. Oh hell, does she ever writhe and grind.

And touch too.

Her fingers have a mind of their own, tap-dancing all along my jeans, playing with my belt, exploring.

It's such a turn-on, her eagerness.

My skin sparks with lust. Desire speeds inside me, racing along as I deepen the kiss.

And she welcomes it, welcomes me, kissing me back so damn fiercely I can barely wait to get her naked.

Because I know, without a shadow of a doubt, this isn't college all over again.

This isn't a gentle, curious exploration. She's not a woman who's simply content to let a man touch her.

She's become a woman who owns her pleasure fully.

And it turns me on more than ever before.

Because I'm not the guy I was before either, with a

one-track mind.

I have many tracks, and they all lead to her.

The things I want to do to her now . . .

My mind runs away with dirty images as I kiss her harder, rougher. Our teeth scrape together. Our hands grab at each other. Our bodies grind, press, push.

In no time, she's tugging at my T-shirt. "Take this off," she commands.

I grin. "I knew you liked to give orders."

"Yes, I'm demanding when I'm turned on. And I demand you get this off right now. Then me."

Laughing, I reach for the hem, tug it over my head, and drop it to the floor.

"Fuck," she mutters as she stares at my chest, her eyes glossy with sex.

"Fuck, what?" I ask innocently.

"Fuck your body. That's what," she says, dragging her nails down my chest.

"Yes. Yes, Lola. That's the idea."

Her fingers travel from my pecs down to my abs, tracing the grooves. "You're concrete. Sexy, ridiculously hot concrete."

"Why, thank you for the strangest compliment ever," I say, laughing, but my laugh is cut short when she lingers on my stomach.

I shudder.

Because fuck, her hands.

She's incredible.

Her touch is otherworldly.

It's better than those French fries.

It's hotter than our kiss.

I want to revel in it, linger on the sensation of her eager fingers roaming my body.

But I'm not a submissive kind of guy.

I'm a take-charge man. "How about some fair play, Dumont?"

"Let's see what you've got," she says in a purr that sends a bolt of lust straight down my spine directly to my cock.

I lift up her shirt, raising it over her head and groaning appreciatively when my eyes drink in her belly, the curves of her breasts, the hollow of her throat. "You are stunning," I say, all gravel and truth.

No more toying.

No more teasing.

"So are you," she whispers.

Roping my arms around her back, I unhook her pink bra, letting it fall to the floor. Then I indulge.

I cup and knead and squeeze those beauties. I dip my face to the valley of her breasts, licking a line between them, then lavishing attention on the two perfect globes. I don't play favorites—I make sure each breast receives equal love from my tongue, my lips, and my teeth.

Since Lola loves bites. Something I'm learning tonight.

Something I never knew before.

I nibble on her flesh, and she moans, a long, feral sound. When I draw a nipple into my mouth and bite, she sighs with what sounds like delirious pleasure.

And as I bury my face between her tits, her hands curl around my head, pulling me impossibly closer.

"I could spend all night here," I moan, but then I raise my face. "But that would be so unfair to your sweet, wet pussy."

Her eyes widen. "How do you know I'm wet?"

I reach for her hand and slide it over my jeans, letting her feel the outline of my rock-hard erection. "Good guess that I'm doing to you what you're doing to me?"

She smiles like a little devil, then takes my hand and slides it inside her jeans. Her eyes stay locked with mine the whole time, heating me up. She's so fucking bold, and it's always turned me on. Even more so now as she guides my hand over the panel of her panties, whispering, "You're a good guesser."

"Fuck, woman. You're on fire," I rasp as I touch her, feeling her wetness through the lace.

"Yes. Yes, I am. So maybe you ought to finish what you started, you *ungentleman.*"

As promised, I lift her up and toss her over my shoulder. She squeals my name playfully, and I love that sound.

I cross the living room toward her bedroom, turning on the light there too.

I set her on the bed and peel off her jeans as she kicks off her boots.

When she's down to only a pair of pink panties, I nearly lose my mind with pleasure.

She's spectacular.

But she also seems to have something on her mind. She holds up a hand, swallows, then speaks, a little nervous. "This doesn't change anything, does it?"

I blink. "Change what?"

"Anything," she repeats emphatically. "We're still going to be friends. We're going to do this differently. We're going to get this out of our systems and be friends. Right?" Her voice is pitched toward hope.

"Yeah, of course," I say, but I'm honestly not thinking about anything beyond here and now.

And I'm also honestly not thinking at all. I'm *feeling*.

And what I feel most is white-hot want.

I peel off her panties and sigh with pleasure at the sight of her glistening wetness. "Look at you, so turned on."

She lifts her chin, owning it. "Yes. I'm ridiculously aroused, Lucas. Now show me how much you want me too."

"With pleasure." I toe off my boots, undo my belt, and shed my jeans and black boxers.

"Oh God," she moans as my cock springs free.

Her reaction is heady. It sends a lifetime's worth of masculine pride surging through me, turning my dick to steel.

I run my hand down my length, teasing her.

"Gimme," she urges.

Grabbing my wallet from my jeans, I find a condom. Then I climb up on the bed and over her, parking my knees on either side of her, my cock slapping against her tight stomach.

"Your dick is hot," she says, wrapping a hand around my shaft.

I close my eyes, shuddering as she touches me. "So is your hand on me."

"Lucas," she whispers as she strokes, reverently touching and exploring my length.

"Yes?" I open my eyes.

"Do bad things to me," she says in a dirty whisper.

"You don't have to ask twice."

I adjust our position, moving between her legs, spreading her open. I roll on a condom, then rub the head of my cock against her.

Her back bows. "God, yes. That's so good."

"And I'm not even inside you."

"I know, and I think I'm going to come in seconds when you are," she says like a woman who knows her body and her needs.

She offers herself up, her hips seeking, begging for more.

But "bad things" are better in other positions. I tease her for another few seconds, rubbing, stroking, until I pull back, grab her hips, and flip her over, doggie-style.

"Get on your hands and knees, and I promise I won't be a gentleman at all."

"You better not be," she says, resting on her elbows, sinking deeper, lifting her lush ass in the air. If that isn't a spanking opportunity, I don't know what is.

I lift my hand and swat her once.

She yelps but finishes the sound with a moan.

I squeeze her cheeks. Her fantastic, delicious ass.

My God. What was I thinking that weekend? I should have fucking called from one of the captains' phones.

Except now I can have her like this.

I move behind her, place my hands on her fantastic cheeks, spread her open. Then I grip my dick, rubbing the head against her wet pussy once more.

"Please," she moans, lifting her ass higher.

I have never been more aroused than with this woman who knows exactly what she wants.

Me.

And I want her just as badly.

I push inside, my mind going hazy from that first delicious feel of her warmth enveloping my shaft.

"Yes," she moans. "More."

"Take it all, Lo. Take it fucking all," I say, then slide the entire way into her, my hands gripping her hips as I fill her.

"Yes," she moans. "That's so fucking good."

It's more than good. It's earth-shattering. For so many reasons, but especially *this*.

Lola is a talker.

As I fuck her, thrusting, pulling back, going deeper, she moans and groans and speaks.

More. Harder. Yes. So good.

She can't stop talking, and it's the sexiest thing I've ever heard.

Her directions. Her responsiveness. The way she lets go, gives in, and doesn't shut up.

"You like it hard and deep, don't you?" I ask roughly as I push inside her.

She rocks back against me. "God, yes. Pull my hair while you fuck me hard."

Pleasure barrels down my body.

Dear God, I don't know how I can last with her filthy mouth, but I'll find a way.

With one hand digging into the flesh of her ass, I reach for her curls, grabbing a fistful and tugging.

Yes. Love that. Turns me on so much.

She looks incredible taking all of me, begging for more, chasing her pleasure with words and moans and sexy grinds of her body.

I missed out on this.

I missed out on *her*.

And I wish she hadn't laid down the law tonight.

Because once with her won't be enough.

I know that now.

As she cries out my name, she adds the most delicious words of all. "Coming hard."

When she lets go, she shakes, trembling, screaming, groaning, and I'm lost.

So fucking lost to the pleasure of this woman falling apart beneath me.

I follow her, the world spiraling away as my own release takes over.

A few minutes later, as I lie next to her, sated, panting, and happy as ten thousand clams, I'm keenly aware that sex with her was a massive mistake.

Because now I want what I can't have.

11

LUCAS

I don't want to leave.

Not yet.

When you've had a taste of the woman you knew you wanted but are just now realizing how much, you don't want to exit like you're wearing jet packs.

You want to linger. If this is all there is before we go back to friendship, I want more moments with her.

I know I should get back to deciphering clues of leading and following, of tangos and dance lessons.

But once I do, it'll be like I'm starting the clock again. Right now, we're still in a blissful time-out, a yummy delay of the game.

No need to get back on the field.

After we clean up, I flop back down on the bed next to her and grab a book from her nightstand.

There.

Books.

Casual conversation to fill the awkward post-sex *where do we go from here* talk.

Even though I know where we go. She's made it clear.

I tap the cover of the book, featuring a sepia-tinted photograph of a woman carrying a suitcase and strolling down an open road, the highway unfurling before her. "*Anywhere, Everywhere,*" I say, reading the title aloud. "As soon as I saw this book online, my first thought about the cover was . . . *evocative.*"

Lola slides onto her side, propping her head in her hand, looking sumptuous with her post-sex glow shimmering across her warm skin. "And when you thought that, did you know it was mine?"

I stare at her. "Is that a serious question?"

"Yes. It is."

"Of course I knew it was yours."

She wiggles a brow, a taunting little gesture, then pokes at my hip. "Aww. You stalk me."

"*You* stalk *me*, woman." I grab her finger and nibble on the tip before I let it go. "And yes, of course I stalk you. I checked to see the designer's name. I was not the least bit surprised it was yours."

"I'm sure you grumbled under your breath—*that damn Lola.*"

"Yes. That's me. I went full-on cartoon villain, shaking a fist at the sky. *Curses!*" I return to the cover, gazing at the image, my tone going serious. "It's powerful. Makes you think. Makes you feel. It could only be a Lola Dumont."

Her eyes roam my face. "What does it make *you* think, Lucas? How does it make you feel?"

My mind slides back to the moment I first saw it. "The first thing I thought was admittedly quite selfish. I wanted to know if you had a new trusted confidante. Did you have someone else you talked to about your work? Another designer you ran ideas past or brainstormed with, like we used to do?"

A soft smile plays at her lips. "We were like two chatty parrots sharing a cage, squawking at each other. *Do this. No, do that.*"

I chuckle at the image. "Yes, I like to think we were macaws and cockatoos, those big-ass parrots that are loud and colorful."

"Obviously," she says with a grin. "And no, I don't have anyone like that. I show my work to my friends. To Amy and Peyton. They're my macaws, I suppose. But they aren't in the same field, so it's not the same thing."

"True. I work with a partner now, and it's good to have someone to bounce ideas off of. Reid is terrific about that, but he's more practical. He'll suggest moving an element a little to the left, or trying a different font." Reid is great at what he does, and I'm glad he moved from London to New York recently so we could grow the business. "But he's not like you. We don't dive into the deep end of how art makes us feel."

She smiles softly, genuinely. "I like talking about that."

"Me too," I say with a contented sigh, returning to the cover, pausing a moment to let the impact of the design sink in. For me, this cover represents the idea of someone desperate for a change, someone who chooses to hit the road in search of a new life. "This image—it makes me think about what I'd hit the road for. What would motivate me to pack up and go?"

"And the answer is?"

I shake my head. "Nothing."

She arches a dubious brow. "Not a thing? Honestly?"

I shrug, conceding a sliver. "Okay. Fine. I'd pack up for family, if I had to. I'd pack up if I had six months to live. But right now? I'm not looking for a new life, or a deeper meaning. I'm content. Life is good. Work is good. I can't complain."

"So the cover made you think that you had no need to take off—that you had everything you needed right in front of you?"

Staring at the image, I nod decisively. "Yeah, it did. I sort of took stock as I stared at it. Asked myself what I'd do. If I wanted something else. Sometimes you have to ask that question to know where you are."

Her brown eyes sparkle, and she nods excitedly. It's like we're on the same wavelength once more, as she answers, "I agree. How do you know if you need to make a change in your life if you don't stop and meditate on where you are?"

"Exactly. And that's what I did when I saw this cover. I asked myself if there was something else out there calling to me, like in this story, and like you captured with this design. That's what I thought about when I saw it. Maybe that's not the answer you want. Maybe you wanted something—"

She grabs my arm, her brown eyes vulnerable. "No. I didn't want a different answer. I wanted a true answer. You gave me a true one. I'm glad it made you think and feel. What more can I ask for?"

"Nothing," I say, setting the book down and meeting her gaze. "You can't ask for anything more when you create. You want to have an impact, and you did that," I say, and it feels so good to talk like this again. Once upon a time, we were comrades in arms, two aspiring artists trying to figure out how to make their mark. Leaning on each other for a second opinion, another voice here and there.

We're doing it again, and it feels natural and right. Like something I didn't know was missing, but now I don't want to go without. She was the balance to my grouch. She helped me see and feel beyond life's little annoyances. And she pushed me to look beyond the practical.

"Thank you for saying that." Her eyes lock with mine, holding my gaze. "And I've missed this too. These little moments. It's nice to have them again," she says, echoing my thoughts as she smiles. But in an instant, her good humor disappears, and her eyes flash with worry. "Wait. This isn't the part where you tell me you have six months to live, is it?"

A laugh bursts from me. "Why would you say that?"

She swats my shoulder. "You just said if you had six months to live, you'd maybe hit the open road. Please tell me that wasn't a subtle hint that you're counting down the last days of your life?"

The thin stretch of her voice tells me her worry is legit. But her train of thought is also highly amusing. "Not that I know of. But," I say, lightly tapping her nose, "I've made a note that the mere thought of me disappearing from the face of the earth makes you sad." I run my finger over her top lip. "Just look at that frown."

"Stop it," she pouts.

I laugh, grabbing her waist and administering a series of tickles that make her squirm. When she stops laughing, I say, "I was just messing around. It was hypothetical. But I'm glad I said it, since now I know you're going to cry at my funeral."

She huffs. "I'm taking back anything nice I ever said about you."

"So that's what? Ten words?" I tease, and now I definitely don't want to leave. I'm having too much fun with this unexpected turn of events.

"Please." She adopts a serious expression. "It was eleven. I said eleven nice words. Don't sell me short."

"Well, then. You're a veritable town crier, singing my praises."

"Also, I'll have you know, I will definitely cry at your funeral," she says, dipping her head, then her shoulders shake and her lip quivers.

I freeze, worry racing through me as she looks back up. "Shit, are you okay?" I ask as a tear slips down her cheek.

She frowns, bringing her hand to her mouth as another tear falls.

Is she that upset about the prospect of my someday funeral? "Lola," I say softly, stroking her arm. "Are you . . .?"

She giggles.

The trickster *giggles* like a naughty little kid.

I narrow my eyes, squeezing her arm roughly. "You are a devil, woman. It's official. Where the fuck did you learn to do that?"

She grins wickedly. "I give good crocodile tears, don't I?"

"Yeah. Scary good. You manipulative feline, you."

"I'll take that as a compliment," she says, stretching, arching her back proudly.

"*Cat* is not a compliment."

"You said you liked my fierce feline."

She has me on that. "Fine. I did say that. And you're definitely fierce."

"And to answer your question, I learned that on my own. My friend Peyton has this theory that everyone needs a party trick, so I decided mine would be crying on cue."

"And how did you teach yourself? Slicing onions?"

"Slicing onions is child's play. All you have to do is read *Charlotte's Web*. Never fails to elicit geysers from the eyes. So I think of Charlotte, and waterworks ensue."

"You are fierce, brilliant, and evil. And you deserve to have the tables turned." I run my finger down her hip.

"What would you do if you had six months to live? Would you hit the open road?" I ask, curious to hear her answer.

Maybe she's right. Maybe sex changes nothing.

Perhaps we can do this whole get-sex-out-of-our-systems-and-be-friends thing.

Because this? Right here, right now? Feels like friendship. Feels like everything we both foolishly cut off at the knees years ago.

She sighs thoughtfully, then stares up at the ceiling. I follow her gaze, noticing the outline of a few stars there.

"I'd travel," she answers. "Maybe that seems so ordinary, like what everyone else would say to that question. But I do think that traveling, seeing the world—that's the kind of thing you should do if time is running out. You'd go anywhere. You'd go everywhere."

"You'd soak in everything the world has to offer," I say. "Live each day like it's your last. I don't think you can do that if you stay in place."

She sweeps her arm out wide, like she's pointing to the door, to the road, to the other side of the world. "You'd have to go. Take off. Leave the mundane behind. Shed it all."

"Live each day to the limit. Devour every second on the clock like they're those soul-selling fries," I say.

She laughs lightly then meets my gaze, her brown eyes soft. "I guess the cover was indeed evocative, like the ones I've seen of yours. I'm proud of you, Lucas. I loved watching you create back in school, and once we stopped talking, it was even harder going up against you in contests and for jobs, because your eye was so sharp, so fine. You always saw the details and the emotions in a design. It's kind of nice to just talk like this. Like we used to."

She was dead-on that sex changes nothing.

We are older, wiser.

"We used to talk about everything. Nothing was off-limits," I say, then point to the ceiling. "Speaking of, what's all that about?"

Sighing dreamily, she hops out of bed, walking to the door. "I'll show you."

But I'm distracted now by the sight of her naked ass. "Damn, woman. You have a spectacular ass. And trust me, I've been ogling it all night, but watching you walk away like that is my new favorite sport. Can you do that again? Like, all night, please?"

Wiggling her luscious rear, she says, "Here's your encore." Then she shimmies that ass a few more times, and my body temperature shoots to the sky.

I am on fire. "Do it again. And again. And again."

She rewards me with one more shake, and I groan in appreciation. "Gluteus perfectus."

Blowing me a kiss, she shuts off the light and rejoins me in bed, nodding to the ceiling. It's not spangled in stars like a kid's. Instead, she's detailed a few constellations. That's all. It's tasteful, thoughtful.

She points at the stars. "When I was in middle school and I moved from Miami to New York, what I missed most was lying on the beach at night and staring up at the sky. You could see so many stars there. Even though it was a big city, there was still a lavish sky. And Luna and I used to go to the beach and watch the stars at night and whisper our dreams to the constellations."

I smile at that image. "I can picture that perfectly."

"When I moved to New York, there was no more starlight, so we chose to make it ourselves. We put stars on our ceilings and shared our hopes with them. We told the sky about art and music, about love and passion. She whispered of songs she wanted to write, and I told stories of how I wanted to make people feel. We shared them all with each other and with the stars above. It was our world—the two of us and the constellations."

The story causes a smile to tug not just at my mouth, but at my heartstrings.

She mimes placing the stickers on the ceiling. "And when I got my own place at last, it didn't feel like home till I put some of the night sky above me. Cassiopeia has always known our hopes and dreams, so it seemed fitting she'd be the one on my ceiling. It makes me feel like I'm home. Like someone knows me."

My heart beats a little faster, thrums harder. "Lucky Cassiopeia," I whisper, then shift closer, reaching for her hair and threading my fingers through those lush strands.

I kiss her again, soft and tender, and it goes to my head. The transition is seamless as we slide right back to where we were an hour ago. She melts against me—not a friend, but a lover, kissing me like a woman who wants to wrap herself around a man.

And that's what she does. She slings a leg over my hip, and I can't resist. I slide my hand between her thighs.

She moans as I glide my fingers across her. "So soft, so wet," I murmur.

"I think you turn me on a little bit," she whispers.

I grin, dropping a kiss to her neck. She smells addictive, that tropical sea breeze that makes my bones hum. "Pretty sure it's more than a little."

"Seems like it is," she pants, rocking against my hand.

Soon she's writhing, murmuring, and telling me to keep going. "Lucas," she murmurs. "I want more."

What the lady wants . . .

"I'll give you more," I growl. I stroke her, touch her, take her over the edge till she cries out, chanting my name. The way she says it, like it tastes so sinful on her lips, convinces me we can have sex, we can have friendship, and we can be back in each other's lives.

We talked it out, we said our piece, and we apologized.

We moved on like adults at last.

And adults can balance complicated things.

I kiss her forehead as she snuggles against me. "Hey, Lo. This changes nothing," I say, repeating her words.

Her brow knits. "What do you mean? I can't think straight post-orgasm," she says, her voice a little gravelly and all kinds of sexy.

I run my fingers down her arm. "We're just getting this out of our systems, and we're going back to being friends. Like you said." I smile, letting her know I'm on board with the balancing act.

"Right. Yes. Definitely." Her eyes glint. "But I'm winning because I got one more orgasm out of the deal," she says in that taunting voice again.

I groan. "Woman, talk like that and you're going to wind up taking my cock deep in your mouth."

Her eyes widen. "You say that like it's a punishment."

I trace her lips. "You look at me like you want it."

She moves down my body, lithe like a cat, kissing my chest, her lips trailing over my abs, her tongue blazing a hot path that sizzles my skin.

She goes lower, then lower still.

And thankfully, her mouth is just where I want it. She flicks her tongue across the head of my dick. "I do want it. I want you in my mouth."

My cock jerks against her lips. "Take it."

She parts her lips and draws me in a tantalizing inch.

Then suddenly she drops me from her mouth, jerking her gaze to my face. "The tango club on Madison. That's where they took dance lessons. I saw them leave once."

"And my dick makes you remember that?"

12

LOLA

"Yes!"

It comes out as a shout because I feel victorious.

He pushes up on his elbows, naked as a jaybird, hard as steel, and sexy as hell.

But I am undeterred. Because we still have a mission to complete.

"Takes Two!"

He blinks. "Yes. It does take two for you to go down on me. Your mouth. My dick. *Two*. Proceed."

I ignore him because I'm bouncing with excitement. "Takes Two to Tango. It's a dance studio a couple blocks away from my friend Peyton's lingerie shop. I saw them there when I was shopping at Peyton's store a few months ago."

His eyes narrow. "For lingerie? You were shopping for lingerie?"

"Well, I wasn't shopping for avocados."

"Did you wear the lingerie for another guy?" he asks in that jealous rumble again.

I stare at him. "Is that a real question?"

"Yes, it's a real question. Humor me with a real answer."

I roll my eyes, even though I like his jealous streak a helluva lot. "No, you caveman. I buy lingerie for me. Because I like it. Like the pink bra and panties I had on tonight. I bought them for me."

His dick twitches. "But I liked them too. So did my dick."

"Glad to hear it. Anyway, that's where they took classes. That's where the iPad has to be." I'm ready to grab some clothes and catch a cab right now.

"Great. How about you finish what you started while I google Takes Two to Tango and find out their business hours."

"Are you serious?" I say with an incredulous laugh.

He glances at his erection. "Do I look like I'm joking? Me before tango, please."

I smile, delighted by his voracious sexual appetite. It matches mine. Because even though I do want to finish the list, I also want to finish him.

He grabs his phone and speaks into it. "Google, tell me the hours for Takes Two to Tango while Lola sucks my cock."

And I crack up so hard. So hard and so deep that it's clear I can't leave this man bereft of a blow job. Because I don't want to stop either.

I lean down and kiss the tip of his fantastic dick.

"That's what I'm talking about," he murmurs.

"Now talk me through it, Lucas. You'll get your reward as you figure out the details," I say, drawing him into my mouth again.

He groans a fantastically filthy *yes* as he slides his thumb across the screen. "It's open," he says, breathing out hard as I take him deep. "Fuck . . ."

He hits the back of my throat, filling my mouth.

"Open at . . ." He tries again, but he can't speak as I wrap my fist around the base, gripping him as I suck.

"In the morning . . ." He thrusts up into my mouth, and we find a rhythm.

I take him deep, and he rocks into me, his thumb fumbling away at the screen.

"At eleven. We'll go . . ." He grunts, panting roughly, finally tossing the phone onto the pillow. "Fuck, Lo."

I grin wickedly, moving faster, driving him wild, giving him his reward.

"At eleven. Holy fuck. At eleven. Okay?" He bites off a string of curses, the last one ending with *Coming now.*

And as he fills my mouth, I'm wickedly delighted that we solved another clue and racked up another O.

But I'm more thrilled that he likes this so much. That he craves my body, my mouth, my skin as much as I do his. It's like a vindication of everything I feared years ago.

That he'd rejected not only the friendship, but *this* part of me too.

I didn't simply lose him.

I lost a little sliver of confidence.

I found it again on my own, but it's sure as hell good to know he responds to me the same way I do to him.

* * *

But when he leaves a little later, guitars and T-shirts in hand, I'm sadder than I thought I'd be to say goodbye.

"See you tomorrow," I say at the door. I'm in a T-shirt and yoga pants. He's in his clothes again, hair mussed, lips full. Post-sex Lucas. It's a good look on him, the lover look. It suits his olive skin, his dark-brown eyes.

"Technically, I'll see you today." He looks at his watch. "After all, a certain someone kept me up way past midnight."

I affect a huge yawn. "That certain someone needs her sleep."

"Same here," he says, rocking on his heels.

The silence of the late hour wraps around us, and for a few seconds, the air is heavy, thick with unsaid things.

I *could* ask him to spend the night.

But . . . I don't think I want to.

I don't think he wants to either.

Because I don't know what waking up together would do to this strange, unexpected state of our relationship. It's as if we're living in a time warp. A day, maybe two, that exists outside the boundaries of the calendar.

If we rise and shine in the harsh light of day

together, what would that do to this bizarre truce? Would it break it? Would we fall apart again?

Right now, the cocoon of nostalgia and night, of friendship and desire, enrobes us.

I don't want to face him, or us, or myself in the unforgiving light of the morning.

I don't want to think too much about what just happened.

The more I think on it, the more I will feel.

He already feels too deep in my heart.

And it's only been one night.

"See you in ten hours," I say, breaking the silence at last.

"See you then."

He turns to go, and my heart pounds angrily, like it's demanding I take that back, like it wants me to ask him to stay.

My pulse spikes.

And I *want.*

"Lucas!" I call out.

He turns around. His eyes radiate hope. Words tango on the tip of my tongue.

But so does the past.

Not just ours.

But all the pasts I've seen. My parents and their pendulum swings of love, hate, and then too much love. A surfeit of love that they smothered themselves in, ignoring the rest of the world.

And the present too.

My job. My business. My focus.

And my sister. That sweet, crazy girl I love to Cassiopeia and back.

"Yes?" His voice is pitched with hope.

I part my lips. "I'll email Harrison," I say, speaking from my head, not my heart. "Like we talked about."

Lucas nods several times, as if agreeing with me is the most important thing right now. "Good plan. Update him. Let him know we're on track."

Then he taps his forehead in some sort of good night salute.

Not a good night kiss.

It's for the best, I tell myself.

If he leaned in and dusted his lips across my forehead, I'd ask him to spend the night.

And I don't want to ruin what we just got back.

It's too precious. Too wonderful. I'd hate to break it.

Or us again.

Besides, we still have tomorrow.

13

Early Saturday Morning

To: Harrison Bates
From: Lola Dumont
CC: Lucas Xavier
Subject: Update

Hello Harrison!

Hope you had a fantastic evening. Just a quick morning
update to let you know we have collected the Star Wars
T-shirts and the guitars. We are on track and should
have everything in time for the security deposit
deadline.

Sincerely,
Lola

To: Lola Dumont
From: Harrison Bates
CC: Lucas Xavier
Subject: Your update makes me wonder . . .

Is this your way of letting me know you want me to make things harder? Is it not challenging enough for you? I can raise the bar higher if you'd like. Just say the word!

To: Harrison Bates
From: Lola Dumont
CC: Lucas Xavier
Subject: Re: Your update makes me wonder . . .

No! It's incredibly challenging, I assure you! I'm simply giving you a status report. I wanted you to know that everything is coming along nicely, and we thought you would appreciate an update. I hope you were able to enjoy some quiet last night. :)

To: Lola Dumont
From: Harrison Bates
CC: Lucas Xavier

Subject: Your updates feed my soul

Thank you for asking! I did relish a silent evening with
my typewriter, my gummy bears, and no one arguing in
the next apartment, over costumes or kale or board
games or llamas or whatever.

Also, status reports are so jolly. I do appreciate yours,
and even though payback is a delight, I'm not so cruel
that I'd ask for more. A deal is a deal. I would never
make you jump higher or through a hoop on fire. Or
walk a tightrope, God forbid!

I hope you enjoy collecting the rest of the items. Also,
while we're at it, did you happen to try the cheese at
Grater Good? I mean, really. Have you ever had
anything better in your whole life?

To: Harrison Bates
From: Lucas Xavier
CC: Lola Dumont
Subject: The cheese feeds MY soul

The cheese was decadent.

To: Lucas Xavier
From: Harrison Bates
CC: Lola Dumont
Subject: "Decadent" barely scratches the surface

Melts in your mouth, doesn't it?

To: Harrison Bates
From: Lucas Xavier
CC: Lola Dumont
Subject: "Divine" is more like it

Yes. I'm thinking of ordering a wheel of Gouda for each of my clients as holiday gifts this year. Alongside a DVD of *Die Hard*. Make that the whole *Die Hard* collection.

To: Harrison Bates
From: Lola Dumont
CC: Lucas Xavier
Subject: Allow me to clarify

By "collection," he obviously means the first three *Die Hard* films.

To: Lola Dumont
From: Lucas Xavier
CC: Harrison Bates
Subject: Your clarification is correct

Yes. Thank you for catching that. Clearly, no one should even count the latter two. They only belong on a list of sequels that never should have been made.

To: Lola Dumont
From: Harrison Bates
CC: Lucas Xavier
Subject: Birds of a feather

Along with *Weekend at Bernie's II*, *Pitch Perfect 2*, *Pitch Perfect 3*, and that thing with Jar Jar Binks.

Also, I like you two. I like you a lot.

See, Lola—you don't have to be all serious with me. We can have fun. Hope you had the fries at Pin-Up Lanes last night. They're divinely decadent.

To: Harrison Bates
From: Lucas Xavier

CC: Lola Dumont
Subject: Last word

So good I'd practically sell my soul for them.

14
———

At the same time as the emails fly back and forth

Lola: Whoa. For a second there, I thought he was serious about jumping through higher hoops.

Lucas: Me too. But I also think he imagines himself as some sort of gamemaster.

Lola: Perhaps he runs escape rooms.

Lucas: Or a live-action puppet show.

Lola: The Delightful Sadist Puppeteer. Which means we're his marionettes.

Lucas: Yes. We are. And I weirdly enjoyed his puppet theater.

Lola: So did I. Perhaps I've secretly wanted to be a sock puppet my whole life.

Lucas: Dreams do come true. Also, props on making that seamless transition in the email chain from serious to playing along.

Lola: I'm quick on my feet.

Lucas: And with your tongue and your lips. Incidentally, your mouth is both divine and decadent.

Lola: I wouldn't know how yours is.

Lucas: That needs to change.

15

LOLA

"I had three hundred and fifty-two new subscribers last week." Peter straightens his shoulders and shoots me a proud smile over his steaming mug of coffee.

I hold up a hand to high-five. He smacks back. "That's what I like to hear," I say, as we study the newest set of designs for his YouTube channel at the ungodly hour of nine a.m.

Thanks, Luna.

Screw that morning exercise shit on a Saturday. I woke up at the last possible minute, showered in record time, and emailed with Harrison and Lucas, while also texting Lucas, as I dried my hair. Multitasking for the win. Then I hightailed it here in the nick of time.

As we review the next set of concepts, I take a drink of my black coffee, one sugar, stifling a yawn.

My client arches a brow, his cool blue eyes curious. "Late night, Lola?"

I laugh. "A little bit."

He shoots me an *I'm waiting* look, tapping his foot impatiently on the coffee shop's tile floor.

I shake my head. "I don't kiss and tell."

"So you *did* kiss. Interesting," the lean and lanky man says with a sly grin.

I wag a finger. "Nope. You're getting nothing from me. I was just out with a friend," I say, since that's one way of referring to Lucas now, and I'm damn glad I can call him that again.

Peter nods, vociferously agreeing. "I'm *sure. Just a friend.* Like, say, exactly how I see Karen," he says, naming his ex-girlfriend and the reason he's intent on growing his YouTube channel.

I know the story well. When Peter first hired me, he held nothing back. The man poured his heart out in a veritable deluge. "I've been racing around the city on rollerblades, playing chicken with cars, darting past pedestrians at race-car speeds, thinking it will somehow soothe my savage heart. It hasn't. Not one bit. See, my girlfriend ditched me because she was embarrassed about my sport. She thinks I'm not acting my age. That I behave like a teenager. *I can't believe you're still going around the city on roller skates*, she said, even though she knows they're called 'blades.' She said *rollerblading is sooo yesterday*. And now I want to prove to her that rollerblading isn't outdated. That it's cool again. It's retro hip, like elbow patches and newsboy caps. My brother says I'm crazy, but I know he's wrong. That's why I need your graphics to help make my channel amazing and sophisticated. More about the art of blading than the speed."

My heart ached for him. I doubted that growing a YouTube channel would win back a woman who'd callously tossed aside a man simply because she disliked his sport. "Are you sure that's what you want to do? Grow it to win her back?" I'd asked.

"Positive."

"We could also try to grow it for its own sake," I'd offered.

"And that'll help me win her back."

Who was I to argue with his heart?

Especially since he seems happier now that he's recording his exploits and triple axels for video consumers around the globe.

Rollerblading is his passion, and he wants to share it with the world, maybe as a way to win Karen back, or maybe because sharing his passion is healing his heart.

That's my hope for him.

I offer him a genuine smile. "Karen doesn't know what she's missing," I say, gesturing to the screen and his antics last night when he executed a lightning-fast fishtail in the park, followed by a precise figure eight.

He takes a gulp of the coffee, shaking his head. "Don't try to distract me. Who's the late-night fella? Is he one of your Latin lovers?"

I drop my jaw. "Hey! Way to pigeonhole me."

He rolls his eyes. "Fabian, Alejandro, that guy from college from Brazil. C'mon. I don't think I'm pigeonholing you. You clearly have a type. We all do.

Just like my type is an ex who won't give me the time of day. Evidently, I like to suffer. So, who is he?"

Even though Peter has become something of a confidante, I'm not ready to let on about Lucas, and definitely not with a client. Still, I can give him a little nugget. Besides, it feels good to talk about last night. "I saw the guy from college. We've been *tasked* with picking up a bunch of things for our siblings, who were tossed out of their apartment but can't get them because they're on tour."

A perplexed look falls across his face. "Does not compute."

"It's a long story." I wave a hand, not wanting to dig into the details. "But Lucas and I were sort of thrust together to pick up the dirty laundry of our little brother and sister. And we had an interesting time running about the city."

"*Interesting*," he says, mulling over the adjective. "Interesting is good."

"I'm weirdly looking forward to seeing him in a little while."

"Why is that weird though?"

"Because I don't know where we go next or what we're supposed to be. I don't know what happens after we finish this to-do list."

He taps his chin. "That's always the question, isn't it? We always want to know what's coming around the bend."

"But we don't get to know," I say.

He shakes his head a little forlornly. "We definitely don't get to know."

We spend the rest of the meeting firming up the design plans, and when I say goodbye, it hits me that I don't feel guilty I pushed this client meeting back to this morning.

Last night, I was annoyed I had to rearrange my schedule.

But this morning, I can see around the bend with my twenty-twenty hindsight. Canceling gave me the chance to reconnect with an old friend.

And to help my sister, I remind myself, as I walk across the city.

I'm definitely meeting him in an hour or so to help my sister.

* * *

For the record, I have no choice.

Not that I'd make a different one.

But I head to Doctor Insomnia's to share news of my evening at the command of two queens—my two best friends.

They peppered me with a barrage of texts this morning, demanding my presence and a full report. From their messages last night, I knew I'd be serving up a plate of details to go with their morning coffee, but nerves scamper inside my chest. After years of Lucas playing a starring role on my dartboard, will last night's turn of events make me seem like a pushover? One hot kiss and I flip-flop?

Only, I don't feel like I gave in to something I'll regret. Nor do I feel like last night was a mistake. If anything, I wish we'd made up sooner.

I steel myself, though, because girlfriends don't always forgive exes—or pseudo exes—as quickly as the one sleeping with the ex does. I head into the coffee shop to find them huddled on a couch with mugs, laughing brightly. When they look up, I simply smile.

Like the Mona Lisa.

And it gives everything away.

"Get over here right now and tell us everything," Amy commands, stabbing the cushion on the couch and staring at me over the top of her red glasses.

"Spill," Peyton seconds.

"And start with whether that dirty-girl grin on your face means I should take him off the hate list," Amy says, miming crumpling up a sheet of paper and tossing it away.

I nod, grinning. "Definitely. We cleared the air," I say, telling them what he said about our *not-date* ten years ago, how he apologized and wished he had groveled and asked for another chance, and how I admitted I should have tried harder to stay friends. "And once we talked it out, we realized we'd both made mistakes and we both wanted a fresh start. I felt like this huge weight had lifted. Like all the annoyance I'd been holding on to was just gone. Poof."

"It's good to be able to let go," Amy says with a sympathetic smile.

I breathe a sigh of relief. "I'm so glad you don't think I'm a pushover. I was a little worried you'd berate me."

Peyton scoffs. "You? A pushover? You're the opposite. And for the record, I never thought what happened between you two was so horrible—well, except for losing the friendship. It always seemed like there had to be a reasonable explanation."

"Most arguments usually have reasonable explanations," Amy adds. "We just aren't always ready to hear them at the time."

"I don't think either one of us was reasonable back then," I say.

Amy shakes her head. "You were both full of fire and pride and raw emotions."

I stay quiet, not entirely admitting how many wild emotions were swirling inside me then. I didn't admit it to Lucas last night either.

But Amy won't let me get away with a noncommittal answer. Her eyes are piercing as she meets my gaze. "Lo, you really cared about him. You had feelings for him. That's why it hurt."

My heart squeezes at her words. There's no point pretending with my friends. "Yes. Fine, I did have feelings for him," I say, speaking honestly. "And that's probably why I carried the hurt around for so long, nursing it like a houseplant."

"You watered it regularly," Peyton says with a soft smile. "We helped you water it if you needed to. But now you don't. That's good. Life goes on, and we move on and forgive."

"And sometimes I guess we forgive ourselves," I say, sinking back into the couch, mulling over what happened over the years and in one evening. "Maybe we needed to be forced to spend time together to face the past. Because in this flash of clarity, I saw how I should have done things differently at the time. I should have told him why it hurt so much."

"You weren't ready then. Don't beat yourself up," Peyton says. "You were young and hotheaded. Both of you. Misunderstandings happen and can fester."

"Definitely. And you found an opportunity to deal with it when you were ready, when fate forced you to. But tell us more about how it *un-festered*," Amy says, big green eyes imploring me.

With the heart-to-heart behind us, I feed Amy her favorite meal—a true story with a touch of romance.

I tell them about last night, the barbs, the fiery banter, the moment he yanked me away from the motorcyclist, our hands in the button shop, the confessions in the comic store, the glee in finding the cheese shop, and then how we talked at Pin-Up Lanes, and how the talking led to long overdue apologies, and how *I'm sorrys* led to the bedroom.

"It was like a movie. You know those movies where you reconnect with the guy from your past, and you wind up wandering the whole city together? Talking as you crisscross New York? It would be called *One Night Stand-In*. That's how Lucas referred to himself."

Amy arches a brow. "Oh, did he now?"

"It was a joke. It was a thing. We were just messing around," I explain.

"Messing around indeed," Peyton puts in under her breath.

"Anyway, we could also call it *Two Nights in the City* or something," I say, returning to the name for our story.

Amy sticks her arm up straight. "I vote for *One Night Stand-In*. Also, hello! Can it please be a book before it's a movie? The book is always better than the flick. Plus, this can be my next great rom-com."

"It doesn't have a rom-com ending, Ames," I point out.

She bares her teeth at me. "Hush. Stop speaking such blasphemous things."

Peyton chimes in, shaking her head, her lush red hair swishing back and forth. "Book or movie, I say we call it *Two-Night Stand*."

Amy smacks Peyton's knee playfully. "But we can't. We don't know if they're having another night together."

Peyton rolls her blue eyes. "Obviously they are."

I clear my throat, cutting into their conversation. "Obviously we aren't sleeping together again."

Amy quirks a brow. "Why is it obvious? Was the sex bad? Oh no." She gasps, covering her mouth, before whispering in horror, "Lucas is a two-pumper."

Peyton frowns. "He couldn't find your magic button. Oh, I'm so sorry, hon."

"Both of you need muzzles." I lower my voice, glancing around. "He's insane. He's an animal. He's completely ungentlemanly, and it's totally what I want. But . . ." I sigh heavily. "We were just getting it out of our systems. It was pent-up stuff from years ago. Like a powder keg. You defuse it, and then you move on."

"Is that how powder kegs work?" Amy deadpans.

"I'd like to know that too. Because I only know the simile *our lust was about to explode like a powder keg.* Which sounds like you last night," Peyton says, meeting my gaze with eyes full of sass.

I shrug, but I'm smiling, owning this moment. "Last night was good. What can I say? But it can't happen again. Because the friendship is too important. I like being friends again. I missed him so much, and I don't want him out of my life again. He's like . . ."

I pause to think of the right word to describe Lucas, but he's hard to categorize. "He's like a brainstorm partner. Like that person you can bounce ideas off of. Someone who truly understands what I'm trying to accomplish with a design project. Someone I connect with on many levels. And talking to him again kind of lit up all those parts of me that desperately missed having that. He's a friend, but it's deeper than that, if that makes any sense."

Amy nods thoughtfully as she takes a drink of her latte. "I get that. Linc and I *love* talking about books. And having a fellow editor as my fiancé is energizing and thrilling. It's like you're a set of Christmas lights, plugged in and flashing, blinking at all hours."

I smile and point at her. "Yes! That. Exactly."

Peyton chimes in. "That sort of sounds like a good thing though. Especially what Linc and Amy have. That you're both in the same field of work as your guys. So, what's the problem, Lo?"

"It's good for Linc and Amy," I say, keeping my head on straight. "But Lucas and me? We combusted the last time we went down that path. And now we're friends again. I don't want to lose that. Our friendship feels both familiar but also tender and new. Like, one false step and it blows up a second time."

"So the friendship is a powder keg too," Peyton deadpans.

"Yes. I suppose it is."

"But you also still have that wild chemistry," she adds.

Tingles race down my spine at the memories of last night. "We do."

"Which makes me wonder . . ." Peyton screws up the corner of her lips, thinking.

"Wonder what?"

She waves a hand, like she's shaking it off. "This might be crazy, but hear me out. Your sister knows you and Lucas were close. She knows you were briefly involved. She knows you have been more like frenemies since college. Do you think she constructed this whole thing to try to—"

"Get you back together!" Amy's eyes light up as she jumps in at the same moment.

"Jinx!" Amy says to Peyton.

"Jinx to you," Peyton says, as my best friends high-five, then stare at me, waiting.

But I know the answer. "That's not Luna's style. She's not manipulative."

Amy shakes her head. "But that's not a manipulative thing per se. Sometimes two people need a little nudge here and there to see what's right in front of them."

"I didn't mean *manipulative* in a bad way. It's just not Luna's style to intervene like that. It's too much thinking," I say, tapping my skull. "Too much social engineering. Luna is all about this," I say, patting my breastbone. "She's a heart person. So it's not her doing. Plus, we've been talking to the landlord."

"The Happy-Go-Lucky Sadist?" Amy asks.

"Yes. Lucas and I emailed with him this morning. So that's another reason I say that Luna didn't engineer this." I arch a brow as a wild thought descends on me. I point at Amy. Then Peyton. "Unless you two did? *J'accuse!*"

Amy holds up her hands in surrender. Peyton follows suit. "For the record, I absolutely wish I had thought of that, but I did not," Amy says.

Peyton nods intently. "Yes. I'm kicking myself that we didn't adopt the landlord persona sooner. It's freaking genius. But I swear on my love of La Perla, it's not me."

"And I swear on my love of pockets, I am not the puppeteer," Amy says a little wistfully. "Damn it. Why didn't I come up with a quest to bring Lola and Lucas back together?"

"Because we're not getting back together. And it's a ridiculous quest even for you two, and definitely for my sister. So, my point is this. It's not you two troublemakers. It's not Luna. It's just exactly what it is—my sister and her boyfriend being indulgent, loud, dramatic lovebirds."

"And the by-product is a powder keg," Amy adds.

"But a powder keg that has been dealt with," I say, chin raised, holding my ground on this point. Because even though I joked about Lucas's tongue while texting with him earlier, I meant what I said last night. *This changes nothing.* "Because if we do have more than a *one night stand-in*, then we're going to be the powder keg that explodes to smithereens," I add.

Amy's gaze drifts toward the door. "Speaking of hot powder kegs, isn't that him walking through the door?"

16

LUCAS

Running helps clear my mind.

Since the last thing I want to do is think, I hit the pavement early on Saturday. I don't want to marinate in what-ifs or what-happens-nexts.

Reid joins me on the running path with a quick nod and a *"Morning."*

"Good morning to you," I say, and we take off.

He's a cyclist first and foremost, but now he's training for a marathon, and though I have no interest in that kind of long-distance event, running is good for lacrosse, and lacrosse is good for my soul. Once a week, I join him on his shorter runs.

"Good morning, eh?" he asks. "That's an awfully chipper greeting for you. Normally you're only up for a few grunts."

"It is Saturday, ergo . . ."

"Ah, I'm sure that's it. That has to be it," he says in a tone dripping with sarcasm.

But we hit our stride, and as we do, we talk less, exchanging only a few words, the occasional commentary about goings-on in the city, client updates, and the like. The quick pace and focus keep my mind entirely where it should be.

On the present. Only on the present.

If I linger on last night with Lola, I'll be studying a jigsaw puzzle that's missing too many parts, trying to link up pieces that don't fit together and, frankly, don't need connecting.

When we're done, we agree to meet up again in thirty minutes to head to the coffee shop.

* * *

And when we do, I can't avoid the topic of last night any longer, since Reid dives right into it with renewed vigor.

"About that *good morning.*"

"Nothing gets by you, does it?" I ask wryly.

"That or you're remarkably easy to read. So . . . inquiring minds want to know." He leaves the statement hanging there on Madison Avenue as we walk, passing a hot dog vendor who's already serving at this early hour.

"About what came before the big bang?" I toss out, dodging and darting. "Or if there's life after death? Or whether, say, a hot dog counts as a sandwich?"

"A hot dog is definitely not a sandwich. That's an affront. As for the other queries, especially on the topic of *bangs*, we'll have plenty of time to debate those. What

I want to know right now is this—how did last night go, and is it responsible for your *good morning*?" he asks, imitating my too-bright tone.

"That's the problem with friends. They know you too well," I say.

"I'll try harder to be an enemy, then. That work for you?"

"Yes. Good plan. My business partner, my enemy," I say, like it's a new movie title. Then I answer him diplomatically. I don't want to spend too much time diving into last night. Not for my head, and not for my heart. It's easier to keep the conversation simple. Especially since this guy can sniff a lie like a bloodhound. "Everything is ticking along. We found two of the five items, and we know where to go for the third one. I think we'll finish everything by tonight, so I'll be back on track with work then."

He rolls his eyes. "I mean with the woman. The one you pretend to hate."

"Ah, her. Well . . ." I don't say anything more as we cross the street. Maybe he'll lose the scent.

"So you nailed her?"

I whirl around, stopping in my tracks outside a souvenir shop, narrowing my eyes. "Don't talk that way about her," I say sharply, my muscles tensing.

Reid laughs. The bastard laughs. Clutching his belly. Pointing at me. "Oh, that's brilliant. That's bloody fucking brilliant. It took basically less than three seconds to get you to admit it."

Rubbing my hand across my jaw, I grumble, "I didn't admit it." But hell, I did. He got me, and he knows it.

He pumps a fist. "You did. And I knew you were still into her. Bet that's why you didn't mind Rowan asking you to pick up his dirty laundry."

"For the record, I didn't know she was a part of the whole wild-goose chase at first."

"Details, details," he says as we resume our pace. "She's clearly the reason for your *good morning*."

"From here on out, you will only ever get surly greetings."

"Fine by me. But the greeting wasn't how I got the truth out of you. Also," he says, like a dog refusing to let go of his prized toy monkey, "congratulations."

I wave a hand dismissively, ready to erase this conversation. "Not necessary."

"Aww, who's the sensitive one now? Want me to play 'You Need to Calm Down' by my girl Taylor?"

I groan. "You and your pop music."

"You and your college love."

I shoot him a *you can't be serious* look. "I wasn't in love with her in college."

"Are you now, then?"

"No," I say immediately, squashing that notion, then stomping on it for good measure. "Not at all. We're just friends again," I say, even though that description doesn't entirely sound right to my ears. It feels too neat, too easy for last night.

Maybe Reid senses it, since he lobs another question at me. "Friends with bennies, you mean?"

I don't answer, but he doesn't need me to because he claps me on the back.

"Good on you, mate. And I take it you want more than bennies, since that's what got you so worked up you nearly clocked me in the jaw."

I groan from deep within my soul. He's too on the mark. "Why are we having coffee together?"

"Because I'm the only person who can tolerate you."

"Ah, yes. Of course. Speaking of tolerating, we really need to find a woman to tolerate you."

He peers into shop windows as we go. That's his MO. "I'm looking. Trust me, I'm looking," he says.

When we stride into Doctor Insomnia's, I spot a trio of women, but I only have eyes for one—one I didn't expect to see here, or so soon today.

But I'll take this serendipitous encounter, thank you very much.

Even though nothing about the way I feel for her is neat, or easy.

Her smile is, though, when she locks eyes with me. Surprise flickers across her brown irises, then happiness. Maybe she's feeling serendipity's role too.

"Fancy meeting you here," Lola says, waving to me.

I walk over to her. "Of all the coffee shops in the city, she walks into mine."

Lola pats the couch. "I like to think of it as mine, but I'll let you join us."

"Lucky me," I say.

Lucky me indeed.

17

LUCAS

That's it. Our friends are officially assholes.

Lovable assholes.

Their suggestions for the final item on the list— what Luna and Rowan would do with lottery winnings —border on ludicrous.

"Take a cruise," Amy shouts. I only met her a few minutes ago, but she's one of those people who invites you into her world right away, as if she's known you forever.

"They're already on one," I point out, sliding right into the group vibe.

"Buy a shark tank," Reid suggests.

"So you think we should go to, say, the aquarium and see if the Ringmaster left their clothes by the sharks?" Lola posits with an eyebrow arch.

"Not a bad idea," Reid says, before knocking back some tea.

"What if Rowan wanted to buy a baseball team?" Peyton suggests, sounding thoughtful. She's Lola's good friend too, and she also makes it feel like we've all hung out like this for ages. "Maybe they're at Yankee Stadium."

I shake my head. "That's not what he'd do." I drop my head in my hands, tugging at my hair like it can activate my memories of Rowan's fantastical lottery dreams. "What would Rowan do if he won millions?" I mutter. I should know this. We've had countless conversations on all sorts of topics. But every time we've touched on this one, we've joked.

Buy a rocket ship.

Buy a castle and a moat.

Buy an amusement park, that one with the upside-down twisty roller coaster.

I lift my head. "If his clothes are somewhere at an amusement park, I will throttle him."

"You mean you don't want to spend the morning going from Ferris wheel to Tilt-A-Whirl to Death Ride Extraordinaire Upside-Down Cutter, or whatever roller coasters are named these days, saying, '*Excuse me, did my brother's landlord leave his clothes here?*'" Lola asks, deadpan.

"I do like roller coasters," I say.

"Me too," she seconds.

Amy wiggles her brows. "Do it! Go to Great Adventure! Spend the day there. The worst that'll happen is you'll have a—wait for it—great adventure."

Lola laughs and shoots her a look. "Has anyone ever told you that you're an enabler?"

"If you mean enabler of fun, I wear that tag proudly."

Reid parks his chin in his hand, his brow creasing. He raises a finger. "Knowing your brother, I bet he'd have picked a waterslide as the very first thing he wanted to build with his lottery winnings, and no doubt the landlord overheard that little row. Check that water tower ride first at Great Adventure. And if you don't want to, I will gladly go in your stead. I happen to have an affinity for water rides."

"So you'd be a water-ride proxy. Interesting," Peyton says, some sort of knowing look in her eyes.

"I'd be absolutely willing."

"I know someone else who has a passion for water parks," she adds, but before I can parse out what Peyton's getting at, I grab my phone and send a text halfway around the world.

I've texted my brother a few times in the last twenty-four hours to no avail.

I don't expect to hear back, but you never know.

Lucas: What would you do if you won the lottery? Would be nice if you'd tell me. And I don't mean the castle, the rides, or the rockets.

There's no reply.

I turn to Lola. "And Luna? What would she do?"

"Donate it all to the Malala Fund. That's where she gives most of her extra money. She's big into supporting education for girls in developing countries. But I highly doubt the Malala Fund would let Harrison leave stuff at its New York office, so it has to be something else. Something more fantastical."

Lola looks out the window, deep in thought, and as she stares at the street, I draw this image of her in my head so I can remember it. The woman somewhere else. The woman who loves her sister unconditionally. The woman who thinks and feels and wants.

And I want something too.

Something I'm not sure how to name, how to have, how to ask for.

Or what would happen if I did.

But when my stomach rumbles, at least that's an easy want to name—breakfast. "Any chance we can take this brainstorm to a diner? I'm starving for pancakes drenched in syrup."

Lola snaps her gaze to me. "That's it!"

"That's what Luna would do if she won the lottery? Open a diner? Eat pancakes drizzled with warm butter and covered in syrup?"

She shakes her head, grinning as she taps my thigh. "Sounds like your fantasy, Lucas. But I meant the fourth item. *Your songwriting notebooks are where you had the 'Oh my God, wasn't that the hottest makeup sex ever, babe?' and 'The only thing that would have made it hotter would have been syrup.'* A diner. Their favorite diner is about ten blocks away. Wendy's Diner. That has to be it."

"Wendy's Diner has the best pancakes ever," I add, and as soon as I say it, it tickles a memory. "Rowan once told me he had the best pancakes ever there, and I guess that was why."

"We can go there and get the notebooks, and we can go to Takes Two to Tango after, or tonight," Lola says.

"I'm famished too," Reid chimes in. "I could go for pancakes. Maybe some eggs too."

Peyton shoots him a stare, like she's trying to send him a telepathic message, and says, "You're not hungry," in a *these aren't the droids you're looking for* way.

Reid blinks. "I'm definitely hungry."

Peyton shakes her head, trying again. "Reid, did you know I own a lingerie shop? It's a few blocks away. Want to come check it out?"

"Thanks, but I don't wear lingerie," he says, and I chuckle privately because I have a hunch what Peyton's up to—trying to get Lola and me alone again.

"But single women do. And some of them come to my shop," Peyton says, and perhaps she's doing double duty, leaving us alone and ushering Reid to the store to play some sort of matchmaker. "Single women who like water rides. Like my store manager."

He snaps to attention, as if just remembering he's been on a hunt trying to find his girl from Paris.

The possibility that she might be in this shop will surely be irresistible to my friend.

Irresistible but slim, I suspect.

"Yes, I would love to see your shop."

As Peyton and Amy escort Reid to the lingerie shop, Lola and I head for pancakes.

Once we reach the diner and introduce ourselves, a woman with Little Orphan Annie curls tsks at us, holding a canvas bag of notebooks and saying, "Finally. I was about ready to throw these out."

18

LOLA

I lift my fork and point it at Lucas's empty plate. One lone pancake crumb graces the ceramic surface. I stab it and offer it to him, chiding, "You shouldn't leave anything on your plate, Lucas."

"Damn. How did I miss that?" He leans forward, darts out his tongue, and devours the last bit of pancake from the tines.

He groans in pure Food-Network-host perfection. "Thank you," he says, intently serious, "for locating that final morsel."

"I take it you're adding these pancakes to the soul-selling list?" I ask with a raise of a brow.

He screws up the corner of his lips then strokes his chin. "I'm considering it. The fries only needed one try. But I feel that to award such a distinction, I'd have to try these pancakes three times. Three separate occasions."

"Of course," I say, dabbing at my lips with a napkin.

"Like when a food critic visits a restaurant a few times before reviewing it."

"Exactly. You want to make sure these are worth going to Hades and back."

I narrow my brow. "Correct me if I'm wrong. But I'm pretty sure a deal with the devil means you don't come back."

He snaps his fingers. "Dammit. You're right. My brain is in a syrup and pancake fog. No wonder Rowan said these were the best pancakes ever. Because these *are* the best pancakes ever."

"Just imagine how good they were for Rowan and Luna," I say with a naughty glint in my eye. "Sounds like they had pancakes after the nooky." I glance around the diner, taking in the frayed mint-green polyester booths, the white Formica counters, the red metal stools, and the smell of butter lingering in the air. "Which raises the question . . ."

He raises a stop sign palm. "Don't say it. Don't ask it."

"Oh, come on. That's why we're here." I pat the notebooks, then remind him of the clue. "They had makeup sex here."

"Or so Harrison says."

"They obviously did. How else would we have figured out where to go?"

"Maybe they just *talked* about having makeup sex here," he says, a little hopeful.

"You're not squeamish about this, are you?"

He scoffs. "About sex? No. About my little brother? Maybe a little."

"He's twenty-five!"

"And he'll always be a little brother to me."

"You want your little brother to be virginal?"

"No. I just don't want to think about where my brother is getting it on. Especially with your sister."

"News flash: they're doing it, Lucas. They're doing it a lot. I bet that's why neither one has replied to our messages. That whole *no cell service on a cruise* is probably a cover-up for nonstop banging in the cabin overlooking the Mediterranean."

He covers his ears. "La la la la. I can't hear you."

I lean across the table and yank his hands from his head. "You are hilarious. He's your brother. Not your kid." But as soon as those words fall from my lips, I stop teasing him. My heart softens. "You do think of him in some ways like a kid, don't you?"

He shrugs, a sheepish smile on his lips. "Sort of. It's silly, I know. We're only four years apart. But yeah, I do. Yes, he's a brother, but he also feels like mine. So, I'm sure I have all sorts of weird issues when I think about him having sex."

"Freud would like to work with you."

He drags a hand through his hair. "No doubt. But look, I know he's an adult. I know he's having sex. I just don't want to know the details."

And the devil appears on my shoulder, pushing aside the angel. "Don't worry. I highly doubt it was this booth." I pat the seat.

He shoots laser beams at me with his eyes. "You are evil, woman. It better not have been this booth."

I laugh, loving how wound up he is. I scan the small diner again. "A booth is far too public. I bet it was the bathroom. I'm going to go check it out," I say, egging him on.

I rise, and he grabs at my arm. "Are you honestly casing the bathroom for a potential public sex site?"

His eyes are blazing, and as they roam down my body then back up, I can tell all thoughts of his brother have fallen by the wayside.

"Sure," I say, my voice going a little smoky.

"Then I'll join you in the casing."

Rising, he reaches into his wallet, tosses some bills on the table, grabs the bag with the notebooks, and follows me to the back of the diner. Framed black-and-white movie posters hang on the wall—*Casablanca* and *Breakfast at Tiffany's*.

I shoot him flirty, dirty eyes as I set a hand on the door to the ladies' room.

For a few seconds, I leave my palm there, a myriad of thoughts spinning wildly through my brain. Will I fuck Lucas in the bathroom? Will I sleep with Lucas again? And most of all, why does it feel so easy, so natural to even suggest it and walk back here with him?

The answer to the third one is as complicated as the way you feel when you watch *Casablanca*—it puts your heart through the wringer.

Still, I want to know the answers to one and two. I push open the door.

The bathroom is tiny.

There's barely room in here for peeing.

And as I scan it, I know something else.

I'm not the kind of girl who bangs guys in a public restroom.

I'm not squeamish, and I'm not opposed to quickies. But there is nothing more annoying than needing to pee and having to wait ages because someone else is locked in the restroom.

Maybe Luna was that girl.

Maybe she wasn't.

Maybe they messed around someplace else in the diner.

But I'm sure I'm *not that* girl.

Yet I'm also keenly aware I'm not immune to this man, nor do I want to be.

I let the door fall closed, stepping back into the alcove with the posters, next to him.

He's inches away, and he lifts a brow in curiosity.

"I figure if you'd sell your soul to end coffee shop phone calls, we can't do *that*. But I can do this." I cup his cheek, run my thumb along his jaw, and rise up to meet his mouth.

I kiss him.

Soft and tender.

A journey across his lips.

As I go, I record the sights and sounds. I savor the sweet taste of his mouth, the syrup and pancake flavor of him that's more enticing than carbs and sugar should be.

Or maybe he's exactly as enticing as that combo is.

Wait. Make that *better*.

Because after he sets down the bag, he loops an arm around my waist, yanks me closer, and hauls me in for a deeper kiss.

His lips are hungry, eager. He explores my mouth, kissing me like he wants to remember every second of this, like every moment is worth capturing. He moans as he kisses, and he tugs as he kisses too, pulling me impossibly closer to him in the back of the diner.

His hand slides down to my ass, and he grabs my cheek, groaning as his body presses to mine, his pelvis rubbing against me. I can feel the weight of him, the hard length of him.

He kisses harder, pushes more fiercely, like he's trying to imprint his desire on me. Make sure there's no mistaking it.

But it's not like I could mistake this for anything other than what it is—two people who want another time.

Maybe we should call this movie *Two-Night Stand*. Or maybe the *Morning-After Stand*.

My skin sizzles with desire. My brain goes hazy. Perhaps I am *that girl*.

I might as well be banging him in the bathroom. Because we're *this close* to having the Wendy's Diner special too.

That's exactly what I want to avoid.

Somehow I find the will to stop, sliding my hands up his firm chest and pressing gently but insistently.

He steps back, breathing heavily, his eyes hazy with lust. He rakes a hand through his hair.

"Too bad we can't do that," he says, his voice gravelly.

"It's not that I don't want to," I say.

"Oh, don't worry. I got the message that you wanted to as badly as I did," he says, that cocky side of him stepping right up to the plate.

And the thing is—I like this cocky side of him. I like the confident man he is. I like the way he's owning his attraction to me. I want to feel the heat of his fire, because he does the same to me. He sets me aflame.

But that's the trouble.

We discovered last night we have a crazy kind of sexual chemistry. If we keep discovering it, mining it over and over, we might exhaust the newfound supply of friendship.

"Yes, my friend," I say. "I do want to climb you in front of Humphrey Bogart. But remember, we're the responsible ones."

He huffs. "Why are you reminding me of that? My dick doesn't want to be responsible."

As tempting as it is to slide a hand over his jeans, to cup him and stroke him and drive him as wild as he drives me, I force myself to focus. "Let's go figure out the lottery thing. We can go to the tango place tonight."

He glances down at his erection, which shows no sign of abating. "Yes, she's totally frustrating. I know. Trust me, buddy, I know."

Laughing, I tug him by the hand. He picks up the

bag, and we walk through the diner. Out of the corner of my mouth, I whisper, "Your dick is your buddy?"

He juts out his chin. "What else would he be? He's my closest buddy. We do everything together."

"Can your buddy think? Because maybe he can get in on the lottery conundrum," I ask as we exit onto Madison Avenue, where we're greeted by exhaust fumes from a bus trundling to a stop.

"My buddy has all sorts of ideas. However, most of them are X-rated."

I laugh as we walk. "I had that impression."

"I was definitely trying to leave an *impression*," he says. "All the way in you."

"Yes, I enjoyed that. And I definitely would have enjoyed all of it. But—"

Lucas grabs my hand, tugs me toward him, then slides his fingers into my hair. His eyes blaze with heat, like they did in the diner. "I know you said sex doesn't change a thing, and maybe it doesn't. But it also does. Because I want you so fucking much. I would really like to do ungentlemanly things to you with my tongue, and I get the sense you'd like me to."

My pulse beats between my legs, and I ache for him. Here on the streets of New York, as the sights and sounds of the city mingle with my desire, I want to take him up on that offer.

I want to forget what we're doing, and why, and go back to his place, my place, anyplace.

"I would like that Lucas," I say, choosing stark

honesty because I can. Because we're not actually going to act on this in public.

But before I can say another word, he bends closer, moves his mouth to my ear, and whispers, "I thought about you last night. When I was home. I was so fucking turned on still. I couldn't get you out of my head."

The pulse turns into an insistent ache. "What did you do?" I ask, heat spreading over my skin.

"What do you think I did? I took a hot shower, and I pictured licking you. Sucking you. Tasting you. I made you come over and over on my tongue and my lips, and then I came so fucking hard in my hand I was sure you heard me all the way at your place."

I melt into a pool of lust. I'm nothing but atoms and elements, crackling and sizzling.

The image he paints is so alluring, so arousing, that I can't think straight. I might need to revise my ruling on diner bathrooms.

Brrrrrr-iiing.

But that sound breaks the moment.

Brrrrrr-iiing.

Lucas grabs at his phone in his back pocket. "Holy shit, it's Rowan."

The little fucking cockblocker. But I couldn't be happier to hear from him.

19

LUCAS

I answer in a nanosecond, grabbing Lola's hand, tugging her around the corner and darting under the awning of a building, where it's slightly quieter.

"Rowan! What's going on?" I say on FaceTime.

"Dude! How are you? I have to tell—" The phone stutters, and he cuts out.

Shit. My pulse speeds up. "Rowan, are you there?"

"—rup."

"What?" I ask, shaking my head. Maybe the lust has fogged my brain. I can't make out his words. "What are you saying?"

"Service is bahhhd." He sounds like a sheep.

Impatience threads through my body. "No shit. Just tell me the lottery clue. We know the rest."

"Oh. Syrup. You got the syrup one? Because that's Wendy's Diner. Quickie by the *Casablanca* sign. Damn good movie."

Groaning, I wave a hand, telling him to speed it up. "Got it. Got the others. I need the lottery one."

"That Pin-Up Lanes one was. . ." He cuts out again. When he comes back, he says, "Tricky. It was so damn tricky. I'm sorry about that one. Should have told you that when I forwarded the email. My bad."

"No shit it was tricky," I say, recalling with crystal clarity how Lola and I argued over it like our younger halves. "Now, the lottery. What's the answer to that one?"

"I'll tell you, but you got the tango studio? Please tell me you got that one, man? Because I totally need my iPad. It has everything on there. All my music, and the poetry I started writing, including a poem I wrote that I'm going to recite when I propose to Luna. And I fucking love you for doing this. Like, mad, insane brotherly love."

"Yeah, I know. Love you too, and I'm sure she'll love the poem. And we'll go to Takes Two to Tango. Just tell me the lottery answer. Is it an amusement park? Because there better be a lifetime ticket for me to Great Adventure for this."

"No. I'm not that selfish. C'mon. I want to save the—"

And he cuts out again.

"Alpacas," he barks out breathlessly when he comes back.

"Alpacas?"

"Yes. The alpaca sanctuary. It's one of my dreams."

Lola's eyes brighten, and she mouths *llamas.*

"You mean llamas?" I say to Rowan.

"No. I mean alpacas. That's what's so funny. That's what we fought over. If alpacas and llamas were the same things. Because they're not, man. Isn't that crazy? But the funny thing is this—"

The connection crackles.

Stutters.

And spits up a frozen image of my brother's face, mouth open but silent.

Call ended.

Groaning in frustration, I call him back. I need the final answer. Why can't anything ever be easy with him? The phone rings and rings, and I want to stomp my feet and throw the device. "Name. A name would be nice, Rowan."

But Lola is jumping up and down with her phone, shoving the screen at me. "The Cousin Sanctuary! It's an hour away. It's for alpacas and llamas. They must have argued over whether they were the same thing, but they both wanted the same thing. To give the money to the animal sanctuary."

Her eyes glitter with excitement, and my heart handsprings. All my annoyance vanishes. This woman, I could kiss her.

I could fucking kiss her all day.

I cup her cheek, pull her close, and plant a hot, possessive one on her lips. "You're brilliant."

When I let go, she looks dazed, staring at me like that moment was sponsored by left field.

But the funny thing to me is kissing her seems like right field, and left field, and center field.

It seems like what we do every day.

What we *should* do every day.

We should take our daily kisses like vitamins.

No, like breathing.

But she's waiting for some kind of answer.

I shrug casually. "You needed to be kissed. That simple."

A smile seems to tug at her lips. "Fair enough. And now we need to visit some farm animals."

She waggles the phone, and I peer at the location of The Cousin Sanctuary. It's in Connecticut, but not too far away, and Grand Central is nearby.

I google train times. "We can catch a train and go there now, be there by early afternoon."

Lola's eyes seem to dance with delight. "I've always wanted to go there. Every time Luna mentioned it, I thought *I should check it out.* But I never did."

"Then I guess all your dreams are coming true too," I say as I order a Lyft to take us to the train station.

"Maybe they are."

Thirty minutes later, we're chugging out of Manhattan.

But we're not simply blindly chasing a clue. Since we're the so-called "responsible ones," I called The Cousin Sanctuary first to make sure we weren't wasting our time heading out of town.

"Hey! This might sound weird," I'd asked when a kind woman answered. "But is there any chance you have some clothes left there for Luna Dumont and Rowan Xavier? This is Rowan's brother."

"As a matter of fact, I do."

As the train rumbles away from the city, I scan the car. It's half full, the nearby seats filled with chattering kids and busy families.

I lower my voice so just Lola can hear. "What are the chances they're all on wild-goose chases too, tracking down items for friends or family?"

"Oh, definitely," Lola says conspiratorially. She points to a harried but happy-looking mom with two squirmy toddlers who switch seats every thirty seconds or so. Her equally exhausted-looking partner is next to her, a smile on his unshaven face. "My money is on a mix-up with their old storage unit. Their precious stuff was accidentally sold at a garage sale," she says, making up a tale on the spot. "Now they're taking the kids to retrieve their old clown paintings, high school yearbooks, and baseball cards."

"Clown paintings?" I ask with an eyebrow arch.

"You know, those sad ones where the clowns are crying?"

"This sounds like a horror story. Why did you pick clowns?"

She nudges me with her elbow. "You're afraid of clowns."

"Everyone is afraid of clowns."

"I'm not," she says proudly.

"Now you're just showing off."

"And now I know how to scare you for Halloween."

Her words tickle a memory. "Hey, are you still into scary books and stories?"

"I am. I started listening to a new podcast last night about a haunted carnival. It's awesome. Want to listen with me?" She reaches for her AirPods, but I shudder.

"No way."

"You don't?"

"If it's a haunted carnival, there are probably clowns in it."

"You can handle hearing about a clown."

I cross my arms, lift my chin. "Nope."

"Ah, I get it. You like escapist fare. You still secretly read romance novels, right?"

I narrow my eyes. "I never read romance novels."

"Not publicly at least," she says in a low, taunting voice.

"What are you talking about?"

"I saw you pick up my Nora Roberts when you were in my dorm once."

"I picked it up! Doesn't mean I read it."

She nods several times, like she's doling out nods. "Right. You only read manly books."

I mime pounding on my chest. "That's me. I only read *The Catcher in the Rye* and *Heart of Darkness* and *A Confederacy of Dunces*. Just in case the man committee ever asks for my credentials."

She laughs. "I'm calling you on it. You don't like those books. You like Nora."

I roll my eyes. "Fine, I read your Nora Roberts. But it was good. That woman can write. Also, I like *A Game of Thrones*."

"So manly."

"And I like *Our Dumb World*."

"The book published by The Onion? A bunch of articles?"

"Love it. Best social satire ever."

She shoots me a satisfied grin. "Okay, that's totally you. I can see how you'd enjoy parodies about the ridiculous ways of people."

"That's definitely me. Clown hater, spoof lover, and occasional sneak reader of Nora Roberts."

She tips her forehead to a couple of guys a few rows ahead of us who are nursing blue coffee cups, haggard looks on their faces. "Your turn. What's their wild-goose chase?"

"Ah," I say, furrowing my brow as I craft a tale, taking my stab at a story. "Two buddies. Their college roommate went on a bender last night after his girl-friend dumped him. He was sad and pissed, and he tossed all her things around town. Left her stuff in a series of dumpsters." I stop, holding up a finger. "But she called him this morning, begged him to take her back, and he said yes, but now he has to get all her things back right away before she knows what went down. So he called his two buddies."

"Ouch."

"It's a cruel world," I say.

She sighs and stares out the window. "At least we

aren't the only ones on a crazy mission." She turns, then meets my gaze. "But I like our mission."

Her voice is soft, earnest. It weaves through me, hooking into me. Opening my heart a little more. "Yeah. Me too."

"You do?" Her voice wobbles. It lacks the usual boldness of Lola Dumont. But I don't mind because what I hear is a vulnerability—the same tender side of her that formed the foundation of our friendship years ago.

That side of her is what led to all our late nights, our talks, our bonding over art, inspiration, ambitions, and dreams. I hear the honesty in it that led me to open up to her about my family, my brother, my parents. I wasn't raised to be that kind of guy, wearing his heart on his sleeve, sharing all his shit.

But with her, I was that guy.

Lola unlocked that side of me without even trying to. She was easy to talk to then, and now that we've peeled away our hard shells, she's that way again.

The question is—am I still the guy I was before? The guy who launched into self-preservation mode the second the going got rough?

Nearly ten years ago, I wrapped steel around myself when things looked like they were going to fall apart with Lola.

With this woman I was . . .

Even in my head, it's hard to say how I felt, hard to admit it.

But I knew in my heart what was happening then.

Why it hurt when we blew up.

Because I'd been falling for her.

I could easily fall for her again.

My eyes drift down to her lap. Her hands are folded together. We've kissed, we've touched, and we've made each other come.

We've poked, prodded, laughed, nudged.

We've argued; we've grown angry. We've fought. We've forgiven. We've started over.

We can do this.

I reach for her hand, slide my fingers through her hers, and say, "Yes. I like it too. I like it a lot."

She presses her lips together like she's holding something inside. Swallowing, she whispers, "I almost don't want it to end."

I squeeze her hand tighter. "Me neither."

I run my thumb across her palm, stroking, caressing, as the wheels rattle over the tracks, the towns whipping by.

We're silent for a few minutes, saying nothing, but maybe saying everything as I touch her hand and she lets me, shifting a little closer until her shoulder is against mine.

"Lucas?" she whispers.

"Yes?"

"That term. Wild-goose chase."

There's a question in her statement. "Yes?"

"They aren't successful. That's what worries me. That's the very definition of the concept—a waste of time because the thing you're searching for doesn't exist, or is somewhere else."

"Right, but we have three things so far. We've found them. They do exist."

"But we're not technically searching for the things. Well, we are. But the things unlock the money, the security deposit. We don't actually know if he's going to give us the money back when we have all the things. We don't really know much about him except he's their landlord. I googled him and barely found any details. All we know is he's a landlord and a writer. But what if we collect all this stuff and he doesn't give back their money? What if we fail them?"

I want to say that it was still worth it because I'm having a blast with her. But that's not the answer she's looking for. Nor is it the answer my head can supply. My brother does need my help. I do want to help him.

"Let's ask the man," I say, since Lola needs a practical answer, not a heart one. She needs me to be me, not a bit of Rowan or a bit of Luna.

"Really?

I let go of her hand. "We're the responsible ones, right? It's the responsible thing to do."

I grab my phone and tap out an email.

To: Harrison Bates
From: Lucas Xavier
CC: Lola Dumont
Subject: Making sure

Hey. So, we snagged three of the five items, but with all

due respect, how do we know you're going to give Luna and Rowan the security deposit back? Or, to put it another way, is this just a wild-goose chase?

To: Lucas Xavier
From: Harrison Bates
CC: Lola Dumont
Subject: No geese were harmed in the making of this chase

I'm offended! You've questioned my character!

To: Harrison Bates
From: Lucas Xavier
CC: Lola Dumont
Subject: Good to know, but . . .

Sorry, not sorry. Just want a legit answer, man.

To: Lucas Xavier
From: Harrison Bates
CC: Lola Dumont
Subject: And the answer is . . .

Actually, I'm shocked it took you so long to ask. You must be having a grand old time.

Admit it, you're having fun.

To: Harrison Bates
From: Lucas Xavier
CC: Lola Dumont
Subject: Sure, but . . .

We are. But the point is still valid. What happens when this is over?

To: Lucas Xavier
From: Harrison Bates
CC: Lola Dumont
Subject: Have faith

You'll get the money back. And as a show of good faith, here you go. Presumably, you use this email address for Zelle.

A minute later, my bank sends a Zelle notification of five hundred dollars, a portion of the security deposit, sent via my email. I blink in surprise, showing the screen to Lola.

"Okay. That's a relief. Because I was definitely feeling foolish," she says.

"You were?"

"Yeah, like we were just running around for no reason. Like we were chasing bubbles on the beach or something."

"His bubbles have dollar bills," I say, but something doesn't sit well with me. The fact that she felt foolish. Does that mean she's not enjoying this the same way I am?

I return to the emails.

To: Lucas Xavier
From: Harrison Bates
CC: Lola Dumont
Subject: See?

Do you believe me now? Now tell me, how much fun is it, on a scale of one to ten?

I'm half tempted to turn to Lola, to ask for her rating. But maybe I don't want to know if it's different than mine. Because mine's an eleven. But no way am I letting the Ringmaster know that.

To: Harrison Bates
From: Lucas Xavier
CC: Lola Dumont
Subject: Rating

It's a five.

To: Lucas Xavier
From: Harrison Bates
CC: Lola Dumont
Subject: What will it take to get that to a ten?

Want me to add more clues to make it a ten?

To: Harrison Bates
From: Lucas Xavier
CC: Lola Dumont
Subject: That doesn't sound like your thing

You said you wouldn't do that.

To: Lucas Xavier
From: Harrison Bates
CC: Lola Dumont

Subject: You have me on that point

True, true. I am a man of my word. And speaking of words, I must return to them because this gives me an idea . . .

When I set down the phone, the spell is broken. The moment of holding hands has passed. We're no longer two people enjoying a wild-goose chase. We're two people who needed to know there was a purpose to the last twenty-four hours. A purpose beyond getting to know each other again. And we got what we needed with the partial deposit—confirmation we're not wasting our time.

But really, this shift is for the best. It has to be.

Because how can you fall for someone in one day? Hell, it's been less than twenty-four hours.

There's no way I could be falling for her again.

That would be like chasing bubbles on a beach and expecting to catch them.

That would be foolish indeed.

When the train arrives, we exit, but it feels like we're not the same people who handed our tickets to the conductor an hour ago. There's a new heaviness in the air. Maybe an awareness that any feelings might be foolish. I focus on facts instead. "So, the debate rages on," I say. "Are alpacas llamas?"

As we get into a Lyft, we google pictures of the animals, and since the differences are apparent – alpacas have shorter ears and are smaller in size, while llamas have longer faces—we're not debating whatsoever. We're agreeing as we point out the similarities.

When we reach the sanctuary, she shoots me a wistful look. "Guess we aren't arguing anymore. Like we did last night over how we met."

"Guess we aren't like them at all." I fasten on a smile. Not arguing is a plus, surely.

She sighs. "Good. I don't want to be like them. I don't want to argue."

"I don't either." But while that's true, it doesn't feel entirely *right*.

Maybe because I don't know what I want us to be.

Because when we exit the car, we're not arguing, but we're not holding hands either.

That's because you're friends, you dumbass. Be her fucking friend, something you failed to do ten years ago.

Right.

That's it.

I'm fixing the mistakes of the past.

I'm not the guy who messed around with a girl and then freaked out when she only wanted to be friends.

I gesture to the white picket fence surrounding the farm. "Hey, have you ever considered whether this might be a haunted alpaca farm? Maybe Harrison is masterminding a horror novel."

Her lips curve into a grin. "I bet he is." We walk a little more, then she says, "Lucas?"

"Yes?"

"I'll beat up the clown if one comes after you."

I laugh. "What more can a man ask for?"

And, truly, I can't ask for anything more, because we're back in business.

20

LOLA

Things I never expected to do on a Saturday with my pseudo ex, sorta lover, new friend: tour a llama and alpaca sanctuary.

But I'm a little bit in love with the cousin camelids.

That's what Davina calls them, the Melissa McCarthy look-alike who runs The Cousin Sanctuary. "We grew up with both these creatures in Auckland," she says in a light New Zealand accent. "That's why I wanted to work with abandoned, neglected, or abused ones here when I came to the States. So many needed a home."

She ushers us into the barn, along the stalls, past stacks of hay, and to her "lovelies," as she calls them.

A thick-furred creature lifts his snout at us, humming.

"That's Harvey. He's just saying hi," Davina says, then pats the animal on the nose. "He's shameless. Always angling for a little loving."

I peer at the license-plate-style placard on the green gates of Harvey's stall. It says *Want to adopt me? Alpaca my bags.*

"How often do they get adopted?" Lucas asks, studying the creature cautiously, like he's never seen an animal before.

Davina smiles softly, sadness in her expression. "Not too often. Most people don't have room for alpacas, or llamas for that matter. Lots of folks think they do. They think it'll be so cute to get a little llama on a leash for a youngster's birthday. And then a few years later, it's all, oops, I actually have to take care of this animal. Like, with a barn. And hay! And it eats two to four percent of its body weight every day," she says, then shifts to her normal voice. "But that's why your brother and his belle came here. They had this idea that someday they would have a farm and take care of these lovelies," Davina says, walking past another stall bearing a sign that says *Spit happens.*

"Always dreaming," Lucas remarks, but there's no mockery in his voice. More an appreciation for his brother.

Davina glances back at us. "Stars in their eyes, true. But I'm grateful for the two of them. They come out here and help. Lugging bales of hay, cleaning up, and taking care of my little lovelies."

Lucas nods thoughtfully, like he's assembling this image in his mind. "I can see that."

We pass another stall housing a pair of black llamas

nuzzling each other. The sign on the gate boldly proclaims *No llama drama here.*

I point to it. "That's sweet," I say, my heart warming as the taller of the two rubs a snout against the other's.

Davina scoffs. "Ha! They're showing off for visitors. Normally they're screaming at each other. Huffing and puffing and arguing about something." She stretches out an arm and pats one on the head then the other.

Lucas shoots me a knowing grin. "That sounds like Rowan and Luna."

Davina chuckles, stopping in front of the next stall, home to a couple of black-and-white llamas. "Here's Frick and Frack." The sign on this stall declares *The Alpacalypse is coming! You've been warned.*

"They're brothers, but mostly there's no sibling rivalry," Davina explains. "Want to feed them?"

Lucas straightens his spine, his jaw tightening. "Feed them what?"

A laugh bursts from my chest. "Lucas, are you afraid of llamas too?"

"No!"

Davina laughs deeply. "They don't bite." She strokes her chin, adopting a serious expression. "Well, I hope they don't." She winks at me.

"So, they do bite?" he asks, clearly concerned.

I nudge him. "They're up there with clowns on your list, right? It's okay. I can protect you from these guys as well."

He rolls his eyes. "I'm not afraid of alpacas."

"Good, but those are llamas," I say.

"No, they're alpacas," he says, pointing to the *Alpaca-lypse* sign.

"Nope." I shake my head as I gesture to the long-faced animals. "Definitely llamas."

"Then why does it say *Alpacalypse?*"

"Because the llamas are warning us about it," Davina cuts in, slapping her thigh, laughing. When she finishes, she bends to grab some hay. "Animal puns get me every time. And don't feel bad—Rowan couldn't tell the difference either. He and Luna went round and round all the time on this one. Here you go." She offers some to Lucas. He holds out his hand, a little reluctantly, giving the hay the side-eye.

"You never had pets growing up, did you?" I ask.

"No. My parents hated them."

"Ouch," I say, frowning. "Hate's a strong word."

Davina bends to grab more hay when a loud buzz emanates from her jeans pocket. She grabs her phone then holds up a finger. "Got to take this. Just keep feeding Frick and Frack. They like hay."

She wanders toward the end of the barn.

I tip my forehead to the bale of hay. "Want help?"

He scoffs. "I can handle an alpaca."

"A llama," I say with a laugh.

He winks. "I know that, Dumont. Just making sure you were paying attention."

I grab some hay and lean against the metal bars, offering some to one of the guys. He munches from my hand. "No pets growing up, huh? And I'm only just learning this now?"

He shakes his head. "Not a one. My parents said they were dirty, stinky, and full of disease."

"Ah, so it was just a slight dislike."

"Just a tiny bit. Also, now that I've said that out loud, I think my parents were kind of dicks," he says, fiddling with the hay in his palm.

With my free hand, I squeeze his shoulder sympathetically. "Sorry, Lucas. I know you weren't crazy about their decisions. I'm getting the impression you are even less wild about them than you were before."

He opens and closes his fist around the hay. "I don't want to be like them."

It's a simple statement, but it resonates.

It's how I've lived my life too. That's my mantra. I've chosen a certain path over the last several years. One with the least llama drama.

Because I don't want to be like my parents either.

Since we've been opening up, I draw in a deep breath and do that once more. "I feel the same about mine. Maybe that's why I've never been in any relationship that became serious." I'm a little nervous, but glad too, to admit this particular truth. This unexpected quest we're on seems to easily unlock doors to emotions and secrets. Like we're on a road trip, and the open highway is freeing our minds and our hearts.

We're saying things we wouldn't otherwise say. Admitting things we'd have kept tightly under wraps.

He tilts his head inquisitively. His tone is soft, caring. "You haven't? Not at all?"

"Don't get me wrong. I do date. But I'm not out there swinging it every night. I'm not a player."

"You better not be," he grumbles.

I bump my shoulder to his. "Hey, same for you!"

"Don't worry, Dumont. Despite this face, I'm not either," he says with a deliberately charming grin.

"You're not?"

"Does this surprise you?"

"Well, you said it yourself. You have a very pretty face. So, you *could* be."

"And yet I don't carry the player card," he says.

"Any particular reason?"

He shakes his head. "Just busy . . . you know. Focused. And I've dated, had girlfriends, but . . ."

"But no one who hooked you long enough to want more?" I ask, filling in the blanks, because they feel like my blanks.

"I haven't experienced that click. That connection, like Rowan has with Luna, you know?"

"They're kind of crazy for each other," I say, shuddering like the thought scares me. And it does in many ways. I've seen where that kind of intensity can lead.

Lucas has too, and he mirrors me, shuddering as well. Two kindred spirits, understanding the dangers of love. "They are, and I don't know what I'd do in that type of . . . situation," he says, choosing his words carefully, it seems. "But then, it hasn't happened to me."

"Same here. I've dated, had some long-term boyfriends. But no one who rocked my world," I say, but there's more to it. There's a part of me that's terrified of a love so powerful that it could consume me. I've seen the kind of damage that can do. I don't want to watch other parts of my life, and myself, burn to embers. "Love feels like such an all-or-nothing proposition," I say with a sad sigh.

His eyes meet mine again. There's an intensity in his gaze, but an understanding too. "It does. Why can't there be some middle ground?"

I force out a laugh. "Halfway love?"

"That sounds like a book title. We'll design the cover after we finish *Things Overheard in Coffee Shops*."

"As long as it's not a cracked heart design, I'm in."

"Please. We're kick-ass, not derivative," he says, then he flinches, startled, and turns to find Frick rubbing his snout against his shoulder.

"I believe someone wants something from you," I tease.

Lucas smiles at the animal, and whatever wariness he felt earlier has vanished. "This guy doesn't want halfway love. He wants it all," he whispers, then thrusts out his hand and offers the food. The llama scoops it up with his tongue. Lucas's eyes light up with childlike glee. "Ha! That's awesome."

The delight in his expression is infectious. It spreads through my soul. I bounce on my feet, smiling. "Lucas Xavier, you are definitely not like your parents at all."

He tilts his head, meeting my gaze. "Why do you say that?"

I point at the animal eating happily from his hand.

"Because you're falling in love with a llama, and there's nothing halfway about it."

He narrows his eyes, but the corner of his lips turns up as he meets Frick's gaze. "Hey there, buddy."

And my heart—forget warming up; it's simply glowing as he pets Frick. "You so are," I add.

"So what? He's cute," Lucas grumbles. "Want more, buddy?" He bends to the bale, grabs some hay, and returns to feeding.

"You went from wary and suspicious of llamas to in love in sixty seconds," I remark as I snag some hay for Frack.

Lucas nods to Frack. "Same for you, woman. Didn't take Frack long to romance you."

"Maybe I'm easy when it comes to four-legged creatures," I say as Frack hums against my palm, gobbling up the hay.

He smiles. "Did you have pets growing up?"

"Cats. We had all the cats in Miami. My parents rescued stray cats any chance they could. We had a menagerie for some time. Funny thing is, the pets were about the only thing they took care of when they lost interest in Luna and me."

He shoots me a sympathetic look. "For real?"

I shrug, but it doesn't hurt like it did when I was younger. "They loved their cats more than their kids. I guess they're dicks too."

Lucas lifts his free hand and strokes Frick's snout. "Let's make a vow not to be like that. What do you think, Lo?"

"I'm down with that plan," I say, mirroring him as I pet Frack.

We're quiet for a few moments, feeding the pair of siblings as they purr their appreciation for the simple things in life.

"Seems there's more to Luna and Rowan than I thought," Lucas says, his voice a little faraway. "I always pictured them as this hotheaded young couple, but there was more going on. And they have quite the interesting life."

I nod, picturing Luna and Rowan spending the occasional weekend here. "It's funny because I think I know my sister, but I can also see there's a lot I don't know about her. She's more selfless than I thought."

He smiles a crooked grin. "Kind of cool to learn, isn't it? It makes me feel better about picking up the slack for him now and then," Lucas says as he hands more hay to the animal. "He really tries to give back. Did you know he visits the children's hospital and plays games with the kids?"

I smile, loving that image, as I offer hay to Frack. "I had no idea. That's so sweet."

"He's a good one. Total pain in the ass, but total softie too."

"What would they say about us if the roles were reversed?" I ask.

Lucas's dark eyes roam up and down my frame. "You are definitely a total pain in the ass, but a softie too."

"Hey! I'm not a pain in the ass. Or a softie."

"But maybe I am," he offers, a little quiet, a little vulnerable.

"Are you? Both?"

He doesn't say anything at first, then he answers me with vulnerability in his eyes. "I know I'm a pain in the ass, so no argument there. But the soft side—you tell me. You said I was falling in love with a llama . . ."

I study his handsome features, from the square jaw, to the carved cheekbones, to the dark eyes. His hair too. All that lush hair I love running my fingers through. This man who hates clowns, who can't stand rudeness, who embraces directness, who picks up after his brother, and who thinks and feels and listens.

Is he a softie? Is he a pain in the ass? Does he love halfway?

I sidestep, finding a better way to address the questions. "I think Rowan would say he's damn lucky you're his brother." I'm proud of Lucas, of what he's done and of the life he's leading.

He feeds Frick the rest of the snack, then says, "And I bet Luna would say Cassiopeia brought her a terrific sister. She didn't even have to wish upon a star for you."

My heart slams against my chest, pounding mercilessly, desperate to get closer to this man. I'm tempted to reach for him, touch him, wrap an arm around him, hold him, and kiss him.

And there's nothing halfway about that feeling.

But something rubs against me. A soft, fuzzy head jutting up against my cheek. And it's humming.

It's Frack.

I laugh, nuzzling him now.

Lucas glances at the creature, then at me. "Maybe he's falling in love with you," Lucas says, soft and tender.

I pet Frack's head as I gaze at Lucas, my stomach flipping, my heart hammering. I no longer know who's falling for who, or if we're sliding together into a wildly dangerous new territory.

Davina returns, a wide grin on her face. "I see they've won you over. I may have to enlist you on the farm."

Lucas smiles. "I think Frick and Frack already have. And I can see why Luna and Rowan come here. I can see why they'd want to support this place too. Question though," he asks, shifting to a more serious tone. "Did you think it odd that their landlord came here with their clothes, wanting to leave them here as a way to get back at them?"

She laughs, waving a hand dismissively. "Harrison? No. He made a donation when he asked me to hold on to the clothes. His donation went toward that hay right there." She points at the bales near our feet. "Was it odd? Sure. But life is odd, and I'm not in a position to turn down a donation, so holding on to a few items seemed a small price to pay. Plus, he took a tour of the farm too."

"Is that so?" Lucas's eyebrows shoot up.

"I like giving tours and showing off my lovelies. He got a kick out of them." Her eyes swing to the acres of land beyond the barn. "Said something funny about writing a scene where a couple of alpacas chase a guy down the street. I asked if he'd consider reframing it. I said alpacas don't chase people, so maybe the man would try to get along with them instead. He said, '*Good point. Glad I checked with you.*'"

"I'm glad he checked with you too. And I'm glad we came by," Lucas says, then reaches into his wallet and hands Davina several twenties. "Thanks for taking care of these animals."

She takes the money and clasps her heart. "You're one of my lovelies now too."

* * *

After we board the train, Lucas flops into a seat with a loud harrumph. "Four out of five," he says, tossing the bag of clothes at our feet.

"Only one left," I say, wishing it were two, three, or four.

"Only one," he echoes, and his eyes lock with mine. In them I see a hint of longing.

A question mark.

What if we had a reason to keep doing this?

I don't want us to fall out of each other's lives again. I want to stay in his orbit, and vice versa.

"Hey, Lola," he says thoughtfully as I sit next to him.

"Yes?"

"I don't think this is just payback for Harrison."

"I don't think it is either."

"Seems to be some sort of project."

"That's what Amy thought from the start—that he

was testing out a concept. Maybe for a show or something. And it sounds like it, from what Davina said." I second Lucas's idea, but have no clue what might motivate the man behind the breakup letter.

"I think he's enjoying it." The conductor calls out *All aboard,* and Lucas turns to me. "And I am too. I'm not just doing it to help my brother."

My heart rises to my throat. "Why are you doing it, then?"

He takes my hand again and threads his fingers with mine, sending shivers all through my body. When our eyes meet, a flash of vulnerability crosses his. "If you'd asked me yesterday, I'd have said you were the last partner I'd want for this sort of hunt. But now I think you're the only person I'd want to do this with."

With those words—*the only person*—a flash of understanding fills me.

In this moment, away from the city, far away from the hustle of my daily life, and so very far away from my family, I can see myself more clearly.

I've put on twenty-twenty glasses for the first time in years, and I can make out something I should have seen years ago.

How I've avoided love.

Hidden from it.

Run the other way.

Because years ago, I fell for this man. He's *the only person* I've fallen for, even partway.

For the first time in my life, I'd felt something deep

in my heart. Something terrifying to me—a hope, an ache for another person.

That was what hurt so much when he didn't show up that night. Hurt so much that I shut the door on my heart.

I shut it to apologies. Shut it to him. Shut it to the dangerous power of falling in love.

At the time, I could barely comprehend what all those foreign feelings were, or how hurt could get so mixed up with fear that you cut yourself off from something good just to avoid repeating something bad.

I didn't just lose my friendship with Lucas.

I lost my first and—as it turned out—my only shot so far at falling in love.

Trouble is, I don't know how the hell to deal with that now. I can't even look at him because I'm afraid I've become a see-through woman.

Instead, I rest my head on his shoulder and speak another truth, if a partial one. "It's the same for me."

The tango club sign says *Back in an hour.*

I've never been happier to have to wait.

More time with Lola. "Are you hungry?"

"Famished." She leans her nose to her shirt. "But I also smell like a farm. I could seriously go for a shower."

The corner of my mouth curves up as my buddy and I formulate a quick plan. "I'm only ten blocks from here."

One eyebrow lifts. "Is that so?"

I shrug ever so casually. "I'm just saying. You *could* get on a subway and go all the way across town to Chelsea, dealing with Saturday evening crowds and the perils of underground travel." I shudder, selling it to the jury. "Or you could zip right on over to my place and be spick-and-span in no time."

She hums as if she's considering the options. "That's quite a picture you paint of subway horrors."

"It's terrible this time of day. Clowns roaming free

and whatnot. It's really best avoided. Plus, it takes forever, and then you'd smell like a llama longer. Lots to consider, Dumont."

She shoots me a dubious look. "I thought you liked llamas."

"Love them. But llama smell?" I shake my head. "It needs to be dealt with stat."

"I believe that would apply to you too."

"Absolutely."

Wrinkling her nose, she leans in close, sniffing my shirt. "What's this fragrance?" she says. "Do I detect notes of hay? With a hint of fur?"

"Yes, I'm wearing eau de barn as well. Which means there's only one answer."

* * *

Ten minutes later, the door to the elevator closes, and we shoot up through my building.

She flashes me a knowing grin. "This is *just* a shower, right?"

"What else could it possibly be?" I say, flirty too.

With a playful eyebrow wiggle, she says, "You tell me."

"Of course it's *just a shower*. A shower at my place. Besides, you said sex doesn't change a thing," I point out with a smirk.

"Ah. So there's going to be sex in the shower?"

I raise my hands, like I'm shocked. "Whoa. Who said anything about a group shower?"

She clasps her hand to her chest. "Oh, right. My bad. *Of course* you invited me over for a solo shower."

I lift my chin. "Exactly. I'm only concerned about my olfactory senses."

When the door opens on my floor, she exits first. "In that case, I'll make sure your nose doesn't suffer."

Not only does my nose not suffer, my eyes don't either.

Lola strides into my apartment, tossing a glance at me as she goes. She drops her purse on the floor, nibbling on her lip while she kicks off her shoes.

Holy fuck.

She wastes no time.

She walks through my living room, paying no heed to the books on my coffee table, the artwork on the wall. Turning to me, she tugs at the hem of her T-shirt, slides it up an inch, another inch, then a few more.

Revealing a supremely lickable sliver of her belly.

My bones vibrate with lust. "Is that your clubbing look? Something to show off a little midriff?"

"Maybe it is." She shimmies the shirt higher as she heads for the hallway, on a beeline for the bathroom. "Maybe *this* is how I dress for a hot date."

Yes. That's exactly what I want to hear.

A rumble works its way up my chest.

Yanking off my shirt, I toss it on the floor. "Are you going on a hot date, Lola?"

She continues down the hall, looking back at me,

lifting the shirt the rest of the way, only to let it fall to the floor, giving me a sneak peek at—*fuck me now*—her cranberry-red bra.

"Yes, I have a ridiculously hot date in about one minute, and I need to make sure I'm in just the right outfit for it," she says with a little sashay of her hips.

Her hands move to the front of her jeans, and I groan at the sound of her zipper. When she reaches the bathroom door, she spins around, slides the denim down her hips, then sheds them.

I swallow roughly. My throat is dry. My chest is a furnace.

She's nearly naked, and I can barely stand how stunning she is.

I need her. Now.

Bending, I unlace my boots, watching her the whole time as I pull off one, then the other.

She reaches her hand behind her back, continuing to taunt me.

To tempt me.

To reveal herself to me.

Unhooking the bra, she drops it in the hall.

I scrub a hand across my jaw. "Your outfit isn't finished," I warn as she steps into the bathroom and heads for the shower.

"Don't worry," she purrs. "I'm not quite done putting it on. Almost there."

I unbutton my jeans, pushing them down, kicking them off.

Stretching a hand into the shower, she cranks on the

faucet then turns, stopping in front of me. She hooks her thumbs into the lace of her panties.

I'm. Dead.

Just. Fucking. Dead.

This woman is killing me with her striptease.

"One more little thing," she says, "and my outfit will be all set."

I'm stone, hard as a statue, hotter than a sidewalk in the summer, as Lola glides her panties down her legs, steps out of them, and then tosses them at me. I grab the scrap of lace in one hand, my eyes never leaving the goddess as she steps into the steamy shower.

I bring the panties to my nose, inhaling her sexy, erotic scent.

I've never been this aroused.

Never wanted anyone so damn much.

"Your outfit is perfect," I growl.

"Thanks. But you're not in your hot-date clothes, Lucas," she taunts as the water streams down her lush body.

I rectify that in seconds, stripping out of my boxer briefs, stepping into the shower, and shutting the door behind me.

"So it *is* a group shower," she says.

I don't answer. Instead, I shut her up with my mouth, kissing her hard and passionately.

Kissing her like she's mine.

Like she belongs to me.

That's how it feels after this surreal twenty-four hours with the woman I thought I couldn't stand.

But now I can't stand *not* touching her, *not* tasting her, *not* having her.

I seal my mouth to hers and kiss her like a starving man. Her lips are spectacular, and her body is heaven, all silky soft and sliding against mine as the hot water beats down, the steam wrapping around us, enrobing us in this private cocoon of lust and desire and something more.

Of second chances perhaps.

I cup her cheek, slide my hand into her hair, and kiss her like I don't want to stop a damn thing.

I don't want to stop falling into her.

But there is something I desperately need to start.

Something she wants.

Something I've fantasized about.

I break the kiss. "Sit down. Spread your legs. You're going to get what you asked for this morning."

22

LOLA

If there are guidelines for how to rekindle a friendship as extinct as the dodo bird—and there probably are, if I had looked—they might not include tit for tat in the oral department.

And yet, here I am.

On the bench in Lucas's shower.

Ready, so damn ready for him.

Judging from his feral look and the steel of his cock, he's ready too. He stares between my legs as he grips his shaft, stroking.

But he's not interested in playing with himself.

I'm his plaything, and in seconds he's on his knees, the water drumming his back, his hands sliding up my thighs.

"You smell so fucking sexy," he groans, kissing my thigh, moving closer to my center.

I tremble at the feel of him. I can't even joke about llamas or noses, can't toss back a saucy remark. I'm too turned on. I'm buzzing, intoxicated with lust.

And then I'm lost.

Absolutely lost to his touch when he kisses me where I want him most.

Kisses.

Licks.

Sucks.

Just like he promised.

He's intense and hungry as he devours me, making the sexiest sounds, animalistic murmurs, as he goes down on me.

My hands shoot to his wet hair, my fingers curling around his head as desire spins through my body, making my toes curl too.

"Yes, oh God, yes. So good." I urge him on, but he needs no encouragement.

He's a man on a mission, and the mission is me. Eating me, tasting me, pleasing me.

He goes down on me like he does everything. *Passionately.*

The shower rains, steam rises, and pleasure builds in me. I grip him harder, lean my head back, let the feelings wash over me.

With my eyes closed, I give in to everything. To him. To tonight. To sex. To us.

"Lucas," I moan, loving the way his name sounds on my tongue. Loving everything about how my body sizzles from his touch.

How sparks spread through me.

How my belly tightens as the ache intensifies.

"It's so good. God, I want to come on you," I whisper as he flicks his tongue in the most delicious rhythm.

He barely breaks contact, stopping only to rasp, "Then come on me. Come on me any fucking time."

He resumes his pace, drawing my clit between his lips and sucking. My thighs start to shake, and my release hovers on the horizon.

I part my legs wider, needing more, wanting to give myself over to him, to this moment, to this dangerous new land we've traveled to.

Pleasure.

Lust.

Connection.

But it's so much more.

It's everything I felt for him once upon a time.

And knowing that does something . . .

Tips me over.

Sends me soaring.

And like that, I'm falling apart for him, as white-hot pleasure races through my body. I come like it's the only thing I want to do in the world.

I'm not at all quiet, but I don't want to be.

I'm outrageously loud.

I want to feel everything.

Experience everything.

I moan his name one last time, loving the taste of every sound on my lips.

A minute later, I blink open my eyes and find Lucas kissing my legs, my belly, my breasts. Then he stands, steps out of the shower, and opens a drawer in the vanity.

When he returns, he holds a foil packet in one hand, asking a question without words.

"Yes," I say, desperate, so desperate for more of him.

"Good. Because I fucking need you right now, Lo," he says, his voice bare, his eyes honest. He opens the condom and sheaths himself.

I rise, still tingling all over, still high from that orgasm.

He moves me against the tiled wall, hikes up my leg, and hooks my ankle around his hip.

Sinking into me, he groans, a deep carnal sound. One I want to hear him make over and over.

For me.

With me.

Because of me.

"You feel so fucking good," he growls into my ear, swiveling his hips and bringing me closer, like he's luxuriating in this unexpected intimacy.

"So do you," I whisper.

There's more I want to say.

As he moves in me, filling me, fucking me, I want to tell him everything I've learned today. Everything the last twenty-four hours made clear.

That he *is* the one who got away.

He's the man I connect with.

He's the person I was falling in love with so many years ago.

And right now, he's that same man again.

But I don't know how to say those things without them going terribly awry.

I don't know how to give voice to feelings so deep without losing what I've only now found again.

So, I focus on the present as we move together under the water.

As he fucks me hard against the tiles. As he grips my ass, driving deep into me.

It's all so intense.

I close my eyes, needing the feelings to take over, needing the physical to blur the beating of my heart.

Sensations wash over me, spiraling to each corner of my body. I shudder with every thrust, every move.

"Look at me," he commands.

I open my eyes, and I gasp.

He's staring at me, desire blazing across those dark eyes. "*This*," he rumbles.

"I know," I gasp.

"I fucking know too."

That's all we say. Because he's watching me, gazing at me with so much intensity. His passion—it's who he is. But now, I feel that passion for me. In how he stares at me, touches me, talks to me.

Wants me.

With everything he has.

My heart slams against my chest, thundering powerfully.

Because I can see something else in his eyes too.

This isn't the start of something.

No, *this* started a long time ago.

For both of us.

The trouble is, I don't want to lose him for another ten years.

And I'm grateful, damn grateful for the orgasm that grips me, tugs me under, and ricochets through my body.

Blotting out all the emotions I haven't a clue what to do with.

23

LUCAS

She looks good in my T-shirt.

Hell, she looks good in everything, including my home.

She'd look good in my life.

No, she looks great in my life, and I don't want to see her out of it again.

It's nerve-racking. The last time I felt this way was with her, and look what happened.

We combusted, splintered into shards, and we've only begun to put the pieces back together, and that's only because we were forced to.

That's what happens when emotions take over. They break you apart.

The bags of clothes in the living room are a reminder that feelings this intense lead to arguments and splits, to makeups and breakups, and maybe even to capricious landlords scattering your things all over the tri-state area.

That's why I've wisely avoided entanglements all my adult life, and keeping those blinders on has served me well. I have this sweet apartment, a growing business, and a healthy client list.

What I don't have are the hassles and headaches that inevitably come with a relationship.

Something Lola doesn't seem to want either, based on our conversation at The Cousin Sanctuary.

That's why it's a damn good thing we both know sex doesn't change anything, no matter how stupendous it is.

When we're fully dressed post-shower—her in her jeans and a shirt of mine that says *If you can't play nice, play lacrosse*, and me in jeans and a gray shirt—she scans the walls of my apartment, landing on a Pollock print.

She points at it. "Hey! You still like Pollock."

"I do. It makes me think about whether abstract art can represent a thing," I say, recalling our conversation when we first encountered each other.

"I think it can," she says thoughtfully.

"Me too. I like to think this piece represents . . . a lacrosse stick."

She laughs. "You and lacrosse."

"I love it. No matter what. In fact, I have practice tomorrow." Those are two things that work well in my life—sports and friendship. "You should come to a game sometime."

She arches a brow. "Be your cheerleader?"

I smile and nod at her, loving that idea. Then my gaze drifts to the Pollock. Right now, it represents something else. It's my reminder that we started as friends the day we met, and we can stay friends now, no matter what else happens.

I clear my throat. "So, I guess we don't smell like llamas anymore."

"Group shower for the win," she says with a pump of her fist and a glint in her eye.

I rub my palms together. "Ready to tango?"

Before she can answer, both our phones buzz, a second apart. I grab mine and click on the text from Rowan.

Rowan: Settle this for us. Do I look more like a llama or does Luna?

An image follows of the two of them making animal faces—or so I surmise.

Rowan: Luna says I look like an alpaca. I think she does, but she keeps insisting I'm the alpaca! But that's nuts, right? She does. She totally does.

Shaking my head, I hit reply.

Lucas: Before you venture down this rabbit hole, are you sure "alpaca" is a compliment?

Rowan: Dude! I love alpacas. Love them so madly they're all I think about sometimes.

Rowan: Also, that was hyperbole.

Rowan: But I do love them madly. I should write a simile song about loving Luna like I love alpacas.

Rowan: One more thing. I fucking love you like an alpaca too. But brotherly alpaca love, know what I mean? Also, cell service is spotty again! See you later.

Lucas: And I love you like a llama.

I close the text and look at Lola, who's smiling as she types.

"Luna?" I ask.

She nods. "They're arguing about—"

"Alpacas and llamas," I finish, imagining the other end of the debate.

"It never ends with them," she says.

"It never does." It comes out more heavily than I expect. But I've seen where fighting can lead. Today, the tiff might be over llamas and alpacas. Tomorrow, it could be houses and lives.

She swipes her thumb across the screen, then blinks at it. "Did you see this?"

"See what?"

"It's just this email from Design-Off. The competition."

I go to my inbox, opening and scanning the note. It's a recap of the event and the details of the presentation. I read the last few lines out loud. *"As a reminder, the winner of the award will have his or her work featured prominently on our website and in our literature for the year ahead. Past winners have gone on to design for Madison Avenue agencies, Fortune 500 firms, and noteworthy start-ups. We wish all of you the best of success."*

She looks up, excitement in her eyes. "Speaking of Design-Off, I need to refine my presentation. I have to do that tomorrow."

I scratch my jaw. "Same here. Guess we better get this show on the road?" I point my thumb to the door, and she grabs her sister's bag of clothes and the song-writing notebooks.

"Time to tango."

* * *

As we wind around the staircase up to the tango studio, time presses heavily onto my shoulders. My boots weigh a hundred pounds.

An unfamiliar bout of anxiety zips through me, which is odd and fucking unacceptable.

I have nothing to worry about.

Lola and I are killing it in this quest. That's what matters—we're finishing on time. Hell, we're finishing early.

"So," I begin, keeping my tone light, "has it occurred to you we could have a future as career scavenger hunters?"

She laughs, but it's short and humorless. "As long as the hunts center on our siblings."

She seems to feel it too—like time is running out for some reason. But I give a full-court press on the friendship thing. "Nah. We have serious skills, Lo. We could crush it in competitions."

"Then you let me know when you find a scavenger hunt league, Lucas," she says wryly.

There. That's better. Awkwardness banished. We're doing this right this time, dammit.

We reach the second floor, and Lola taps on the glass door of the studio. I peer inside. A woman in a satiny red dress meets our gaze, a smile tugging at her pouty red lips, lighting up her face.

"She looks exactly like you'd expect a tango instructor to look," I remark.

Lola smiles. "She does. She's straight from central casting, with that cascade of black curls, those hips, and legs for days."

The woman reaches for the door handle and pulls it open with a flourish.

"Welcome! You must be the soon-to-be Mr. and Mrs. Abernathy." Her accent contains a hint of Argentina, adding even more to the authenticity.

I narrow my eyes, then shake my head. "No, I'm Lucas Xavier. And this is Lola Dumont."

The tango woman takes my hand then Lola's. "I'm Angeline. I have a lesson any minute, but if you two are here to inquire about lessons, I'd love to teach you. I can tell you'd be very good."

"How can you tell?" I ask.

She waves a hand like she's sprinkling us with fairy dust or something. "I can read couples' energy."

"We're not a couple," Lola cuts in.

Damn straight. "We're just friends. Good friends," I say with a smile.

Lola flashes her pearly whites too. "Great friends. We just reconnected."

Angeline glances between the two of us, her eyes gleaming. "Hmm. Your energy is quite strong." She grins, taking a beat. "What can I do for you?"

Lola bats first this time. "We're hoping you have an iPad. Left by Harrison Bates."

Her brown eyes sparkle. "Harrison. Yes, of course. He said you might be coming."

"Might? Did he bet you a six-pack?" I ask.

She scoffs, laughing. "No. I'm not a betting woman. I showed him some basic tango steps and told him I'd hold on to the iPad if he came back for a lesson."

That's surprising. "Did he?"

She glances at the clock on the wall. "He should be here tomorrow. I can't wait to teach him how to tango."

Something about this information throws me off,

but I'm not sure why, so I focus on the goal. Get the iPad. Finish the tasks. Snag the security deposit.

Be done.

That's what I want right now. To be done with this fickle landlord and his absurd breakup letter. I have work piling up and projects to finish, as well as a design competition to prepare for.

This has run its course.

"Hope he enjoys it. And thanks again for taking care of the iPad. May we have it back?"

"Of course," she says. She heads to a desk, grabs it, and hands it over.

"Thanks, Angeline," Lola says.

"If you change your mind, I'm here. I've taught tango to all kinds of couples. It can be fun for friends too." Angeline smiles knowingly.

"Thanks. We'll keep that in mind," I say, but I won't, because tangoing with Lola won't help me be the responsible one.

And that's who I am.

That's the part I know how to play.

When we reach the street, I take a deep, fueling breath, and Lola seems to do the same. "So, here's the big question," she says.

"Yeah?" A part of me hopes she'll say, *Want to figure out a way to . . .*

But I don't even know how to finish that sentence. I don't know how to figure out anything right now.

She smiles, lifting up her chin. "We're going to do it this time, right?"

"Stay friends?" I ask.

"Yes. We're not those hotheaded college kids anymore, right?" She adds in an elbow nudge. "We let our friendship die before, but we're going to be adults this time."

I have no choice but to agree. "We so are. We are definitely wiser, more mature. We can do this." I muster up all my confidence.

Because we can.

And we will.

Because it takes two to tango, and we both want this friendship.

And neither wants the messiness and the inevitable pain of what Luna and Rowan have. How could they be headed for anything but trouble?

"We're doing it." I offer a fist for knocking, and she takes me up on it like she's one of the guys.

We quickly segue into sorting out what to do with the items we've collected. I'll hold on to Rowan's things, she'll keep Luna's, and we'll both email Harrison by tomorrow morning.

That's all there is.

On Madison Avenue, as the twilight sky surrounds us, I search for what to say next. We've bumped fists in agreement that we should remain friends, but what can I do differently this time around?

I have to make it work.

"So, my good friend Lola. Do you want to have coffee this week? As friends?"

She smiles. "I would like that."

Setting Luna's things on the ground, she then wraps her arms around me in a hug, and I try to resist the smell of her hair and the scent of her skin.

The feel of her in my arms.

She doesn't feel like a friend.

But she has to be. Because we're adults. Because love is dangerous. Because we're doing things the mature way this time around.

I let go. "Bye, Lola."

"Bye, Lucas."

Trouble is, it doesn't feel like a friendly goodbye when I turn the other way, my heart weighing ten thousand pounds.

24

To: Lola Dumont, Lucas Xavier
From: Harrison Bates
Subject: A deal is a deal

Just gonna come right out and say it. I had NO FAITH
in you two. I didn't think you'd pull it off so quickly. I
mean, c'mon. What were the chances? But where there's
a will, there's a way. And I have to know—did you
enjoy it?

To: Harrison Bates
From: Lola Dumont
CC: Lucas Xavier
Subject: Re: A deal is a deal

Perhaps the question is—did YOU enjoy it?

To: Lola Dumont
CC: Lucas Xavier
From: Harrison Bates
Subject: So much

More than I thought I would! After all, I went bowling with a friend, visited some alpacas, devoured cheese, and had the best pancakes in the city. (Guess Luna and Rowan were right about that one!)

Life has a funny way of working out, doesn't it?

To: Harrison Bates
CC: Lola Dumont
From: Lucas Xavier
Subject: So hilarious

Yeah. It's a barrel of monkeys.

To: Lucas Xavier
CC: Lola Dumont
From: Harrison Bates
Subject: Why so sad?

Aww, is there trouble in romance land?

To: Harrison Bates
CC: Lola Dumont
From: Lucas Xavier
Subject: Not sad, just busy

How about the rest of the security deposit?

To: Lucas Xavier
CC: Lola Dumont
From: Harrison Bates
Subject: I'm a man of my word

Check your Zelle! Also, maybe you should take a tango lesson to cheer up. But then again, ask me in a couple of hours, since I'm headed off to mine. Who knew? Me? Tangoing? Well, the jury's still out. I might have two left feet.

But what I do have is this—a clear mind.

There's nothing quite like a quiet place to live to set one's creativity free.

And now I'm off to try out the dance of love.

25

LOLA

I answer Harrison's emails while I finish my Sunday morning workout, but his last note gives me an idea.

Because quiet sounds perfect. After all, creativity is what I need.

Yep.

I need to focus on the presentation, on my new clients, and on my existing projects at Bailey & Brooks.

It's that simple.

The Design-Off organizers said it themselves— winning is a huge opportunity. It can open new doors.

That's what I want.

Breath coming fast, I hit end on the elliptical, step off the machine, and begin a series of cool-down stretches.

When I'm done, I leave the gym, satisfied to have checked the workout off my to-do list. I did it solo too, since Amy is allergic to early Sunday morning exercise. I'll probably see her later after I knock out some work.

That's my plan for the rest of the morning after I shower, dress, and grab a bagel. Back at home, I do my best to avoid my bedroom.

Because I'm not sleepy, of course. I work in the living room, where I fine-tune some designs for Peter before I return to my presentation, digging in.

I focus on the project for a few hours, savoring the silence of my apartment. After I hit my goal for the day, I stretch, adding a contented sigh for good measure.

"I've got the whole day ahead of me," I say to myself, since there's no one else there to tell.

Just the computer screen and me.

Me and Photoshop.

That's how I like it.

So I hop over to my project notes for a book cover I'm starting, a brand-new romantic comedy from Amy.

Staring at the spec sheet, I review the themes, mulling over how to present them—it's a second-chance romance set against the backdrop of New York City.

Well, la-di-da.

That should be a piece of cake.

But as I consider the possibilities, I can't quite settle on the right look. Should it be illustrated? Photo-graphic? Perhaps a combination of the two?

I shoot a text over to Amy, seeing if she wants to chat.

Her reply is fast and furious.

Amy: Would love to see you later! Linc and I are going to Brooklyn to see the shopping cart races with Baldwin and James. Then I have to grab a drink with an agent who wants to send me an exclusive submission later this week. A new comedy! Gah! I love exclusive submissions, almost as much as I love shopping cart races. But maybe we can do something tomorrow?

Lola: Of course. Have fun.

I stare at the exchange, furrowing my brow, wondering why it feels empty somehow. This is a perfectly normal exchange with my friend.

My friend who is busy with her fiancé.

But that's normal. It doesn't bother me. So then what's this spark of tension shooting through my shoulders, and why does my pulse spike with nerves?

That's odd. Why would I be nervous or worried? I'm not an anxious person.

And yet, the quiet feels cloying, like it's sticking to me, a perfume that's lingered too long.

Maybe the strange presence is coming from the bedroom.

Nope. Don't want to go there, literally or metaphorically.

In fact, I need to get out of here. And perhaps I need company—to discuss this cover with.

Peyton's not in the same field, but no matter. She has a great eye for pretty things.

I fire off a text, asking what she's up to.

Peyton: Tristan and I are taking Barrett and a friend to the movies later tonight. But first, inventory. Admit it: you're dying to come to my store and help Marley and me with inventory.

I consider her note. Inventory? Sure. Sounds like a better way to spend the rest of my Sunday afternoon than avoiding the room where I started to let Lucas into my heart.

* * *

Note to self: inventory is the opposite of fun.

Fortunately, I arrive at the tail end of it.

The gals are nearly done—just cataloging one more item.

I hold up a silky red bra for Peyton and Marley. "How about this sexy thing?"

"Ooh, that's a dazzling one," Marley says, eyes widening as she gawks at the lingerie. "I wore something like that in sapphire blue last night."

I take a closer look at the lace. "Come to think of it, this reminds me of the—"

I stop because I don't want to say that out loud. It reminds me of Lucas, and what I wore last night with him.

A bra he couldn't stop staring at. A bra I loved taking off for him when I stripped on the way to the shower. A shiver runs through me at the white-hot memory—the sweet agony of his touch and the exquisite sensations that raced through me when he kissed me everywhere.

The bone-deep connection I felt with the man.

I won't belittle my heart by saying it was *just sex.*

It wasn't *just sex* whatsoever.

But that's beside the point.

"Earth to Lola." Peyton waves a hand in front of my face.

I snap my gaze up. "Sorry. I drifted off."

"Yes, I know inventory is not that thrilling. That's why we always have a drink after. Besides," Peyton says, shooting Marley a knowing glance, "I want to hear more about what you did in your dazzling sapphire-blue lingerie."

Marley adopts an overly demure smile. "Who said it was dazzling?"

"Um, you did." Peyton points at the brunette. "Might it have involved a certain someone you met yesterday?"

"Maybe it did," she trails off and adds a flirty little grin.

That piques my interest, and when the three of us head to Gin Joint to grab some libations, I wait until we order and then command playfully, "Tell us, Marley. Dare I say *dazzle* us?"

As we drink, Marley shares a few details and I lean closer, doing my best to stay in the present moment. It's a scintillating tale, but I have to work to focus on the details.

Because the moment I want to be in is *my* last night. *My* yesterday. My twenty-four hours with Lucas.

Except that's not how we fix mistakes.

We repair the past with a better present.

By doing things right this time around.

And as it happens, I'm not technically any closer to figuring out the design issues of my new book cover. So maybe, just maybe, I should see if Lucas wants to help.

When Marley and Peyton grab refills at the bar, I fire off a text.

Lola: Hey! Want to grab that coffee tomorrow? I could use your brain.

Lucas: My brain is at your disposal.

26

LUCAS

I'd like other parts to be at her disposal too.

Not just *that* part.

All the parts. Except that's not in the cards, so I shove those annoying, irresponsible, nagging notions of romance and a future and *I'm falling for you* into the corner, then I stomp them pancake-flat and light them on fire for good measure.

There.

I wipe my hands of emotions, falling, love, and all those other dangerous ideas.

Besides, I have plenty to deal with.

Like the fact that our office space still isn't ready.

Like the work I fell behind on over the weekend.

Like the presentation.

That's my Monday.

And all day long as I refine my work, I check the clock. I check it religiously. I check it like *it's* my motherfucking job.

And when the clock ticks closer to coffee time, I close the laptop, head home, and change into a T-shirt I know she'll like. I run my fingers through my hair and head to the coffee shop.

This is good. Everything we fucked up last time, we are unfucking now.

We are such goddamn adults we should earn medals for excellence in adulting.

And really, isn't that everything I've ever wanted?

The second I open the door to Doctor Insomnia's, my heart springs out of my chest, scampering to her.

What the hell?

I grab the outlaw organ, stuff it back between my lungs, and tell it to settle the hell down.

This is not the time or place for stupid displays of affection.

Yet as I head over to her, there's a smile on my face that I can't hide. My skin warms, my pulse races, and my mind is surfing a dopamine wave just being near her.

She stands and smiles too, and then *it* happens.

The awkward sets in.

We're a foot away from each other, and I don't know if we should hug, or shake hands, or something else.

"Hey, you," she says, going first, a note of sweetness in that last word that winds its way around my heart, tugging it perilously close to her.

"Hey there." I don't know if I should respond to the sound or the situation. Where is this covered in the rules we laid down?

"Good to see you," she says, shifting to full-on friends mode. Pursing her lips, she draws a breath then wraps me in a hug. "Thanks for letting me borrow your brain."

Ah, yes. The situation. Focus on that. "You've got all access. Twenty-four seven," I say, turning my nose away from her hair because if I spend too long inhaling her fantastic scent, I will backslide.

Hell, I'll relapse into offers of group showers and sleepovers and breakfasts, and spending every single second with her, like I stupidly want to.

We separate and sit. She clears her throat, gesturing to the empty table in front of me. "Want a coffee?"

"Sure. Yeah. Definitely. Coffee is good." I sound like an overeager teenager on a first date. I gesture with my thumb to the counter. "I'll go grab one."

I tell myself to *be cool* as I wait for the drink.

And maybe I listen.

After I snag a coffee, I return to her, nodding at her mug. "Coffee. One sugar." I tap my temple. "I remember."

She shrugs happily. "Some things never change."

But some things do.

And we're one of those things.

I take a drink, set down the mug, and rub my hands together. "All right, let's do this."

She tells me the cover concept, and we spend the

next thirty minutes tossing around ideas, sketching out possibilities, and brainstorming.

It's stimulating and fantastic, and I love every second.

I've missed this. I've missed her. I've missed the camaraderie. I lost this for nearly ten years, and I don't want to give it up again, no matter how much I long to touch her.

That's what I need to keep in mind. Not how cute she looks when she is concentrating and nibbling on the corners of her lips. I could lick that lip.

That's just the kind of thinking that got us into trouble before.

Just focus on the present.

I lean back in my chair, and because the present is pretty damned good, I say, "We should do this again."

"We should definitely do it again," she says, her tone cheery.

"How about tomorrow? Same time?"

"It's a plan."

Right.

A plan, not a date.

When I leave, I give her another hug, and for a moment, I consider the risk of hauling her in for a hot, wet kiss that could turn into a long, sweaty night together.

But I don't.

And I'm both happy and miserable at the same time.

27

LOLA

When you're friends again with the guy you like a whole helluva lot, you get to do super-fun things like analyzing every text you want to send him to make sure you're not crossing a line.

For instance, this one:

Lola: At MOMA right now. Staring at *Starry Night*. This painting makes me feel all the things.

But nope. You can't send that because what if he thinks you're feeling all the things for him?

So you try another time:

Lola: Just walked past Wendy's Diner on the way to

work. By the way, we should try the silver-dollar pancakes. I hear they're spectacular.

But that stays in the drafts too, because what if "silver dollar" is a new euphemism for, I dunno, a bathroom bang? These are the hurdles a modern woman attempting to navigate a rekindled friendship has to face.

The challenges compound when I see him again and it's terrific and painful and utterly unhelpful.

It's Tuesday, and we meet at the Pin-Up Lanes bowling alley and play a game, catching up on our favorite music and trading stories about our zaniest clients.

I tell him about Peter the Blade, and he tells me about a woman he and Reid worked for who they called the Stickler.

"And that was an understatement," he says, then he picks up a ball and effortlessly throws a strike.

"Woo-hoo!" I shout—because strikes are impressive and deserve a cheer, even when it's the competition nailing them.

He blows on his fingers. "When you've got it, you've got it."

"And you definitely have it," I say with a saucy wink.

And like that, his brown eyes flame.

My skin heats.

But we're out-of-bounds.

That's another obstacle in this resurrected friendship. If you slip into innuendo, you have to dial it back, cool it off, and zip it up.

I'm still hopscotching around the heat on Wednesday when we meet for a drink after work, hitting Gin Joint this time.

I'm armed and ready with innocuous topics, but as soon as I fire away with the first one, I realize it's not innocuous whatsoever.

"Did you hear about Reid and Marley?" I ask.

He wiggles his brow. "I got the gist of it. Didn't expect that."

"I know, right?" I say with a grin. "But I guess—"

Then I stop myself, because talking about the two of them is not going to keep my mind in the friend zone.

It's going to send me spinning into the *let's try again* zone.

I execute a one-eighty, and we spend the next hour talking about Luna and Rowan. Cell service is still spotty for them, but we've gotten occasional updates, and their tour is going well.

When the night ends, that thing happens again.

That awkward thing where we stand on the street, rock on our heels, and don't say, *Fuck it, let's go home together.*

Instead, I rise up on my tiptoes, plant a kiss on his cheek, and say, "See you at the competition."

"See you Friday, Lo," he says, and when I return home, I trudge up the stairs, kick off my boots, and flop on the couch. I grab a book, but after a few pages, I toss it because I can't retain a damn word.

I grab a blanket from the arm of the sofa and curl up under it, because I can't stand being in the bedroom.

I haven't been able to stand it since we spent the night together.

I reach for my phone, but when I reread the email from the design committee, I feel nothing.

Not a thing.

Not an ounce.

The same applies the next day, and on into Friday.

That morning, I shower, dress, and head to work, trying to psych myself up about tonight.

Or about the haunted carnival podcast, because spooky shit is going down behind the Ferris wheel.

Or about Luna's exclamation-point-laden text with the news that the Love Birds were invited on another honeymoon cruise.

Or even about Peter's enthusiastic email that arrives when I reach the office.

My channel is crushing it! Views are up, comments are bonkers, and I nabbed a sponsor. Also, big news! The ex doesn't want me back, and I don't care because I met a lady blader in the park. This might sound crazy, and of course my brother says it's impossible . . . but it just feels right. It's been a whirlwind in just twenty-four hours. But sometimes that's how it goes!

Fine, I *am* excited about Peter's turnaround in his fortunes, and in his attitude too.

But I'm also insanely jealous of him as I ride the elevator up to my stop at Bailey & Brooks.

I reply, letting him know how happy—and not how envious—I am for him. What I want to say, but don't, is that it doesn't sound impossible at all, and sometimes you can totally fall for someone in twenty-four hours.

Give or take ten years.

In my office, I jump into the pool of book covers, swimming in ideas and designs.

I spend the morning working on the new romantic comedy, and it's singing, thanks to Lucas's feedback from the other night.

But my heart pinches when I think about him, and I'm caught up in a wave of missing him. A wave so punishing it feels like I've been pummeled by the ocean.

Which is silly, since I just saw him the other night.

And I'll see him again tonight at the awards ceremony.

I shake it off, focusing on the presentation.

A little before lunch, Amy pops into my office with a delighted glint in her green eyes. "Knock, knock."

"Come in."

She cups the side of her mouth, then whispers, "Word on the street is that Baldwin is going to ask James to marry him this weekend."

She does a little happy dance in the doorway, and I

try—I swear, I try so hard—to get excited for our friend Baldwin.

I love good news and romance, and I love little nuggets of intel about colleagues, especially Baldwin, who is a fantastic guy.

But I'm a blank person.

I slap on a grin that feels plastic. "That's great."

Amy stares daggers at me. "That's great?"

"Of course," I say.

Amy shakes her head, heaves a sigh, and parks her palms on my desk. "It's not great, Lola. It's stupendous. No. It's more. It's life-affirming, love-affirming, shout-to-the-heavens news."

She's right.

She's so damn right.

When she puts it like that, my dumb heart cracks open. Wide and brutally. My throat tightens, and without warning, I burst into tears.

In a second, Amy shuts the door to my office, rounds my desk, and kneels next to me. "Sweetie, what's wrong?"

Sobbing, I cry some more, then choke out the painful words that constrict my throat. "I don't want to be just friends with Lucas."

She sighs sympathetically, then rubs my arm. "Of course you don't. You want him to be your person."

I nod, sniffling at the ease of her understanding, the simplicity of her pronouncement. "I do. Isn't that stupid? It's so stupid because it won't happen, and we agreed to be friends because we were so dumb last time, and so foolish and young. And I don't want to be foolish and young. I want to be smart and mature."

She takes a beat, then asks softly, "How's that working out for you?"

A fresh, hot well of tears rises up and falls from my eyes. I drop my head in my hands. "I hate everything."

She laughs, but it's a loving laugh. "That's the issue. You're not a hater, Lola. You're a lover. You're a smart, vibrant, strong woman. The last thing you are is a hater. But you're also stubborn."

I raise my face, letting her truth weave its way into my heart. She's more than right. She's bull's-eye accurate, and I can't hide from the truth anymore. "And afraid. Don't forget afraid."

She takes my hand, squeezes it. "But you don't have to be afraid. You don't have to be scared you'll be like your parents, blinded by love. And you don't have to be like your sister, a wonderful but loose cannon."

"I don't have to," I say, nodding, agreeing, feeling.

Because she's right. Holy smokes. She's so damn right.

I don't have to make their choices. I can love without losing my humanity, without losing myself.

I can love, not how they love, but like myself, with my whole heart and my head too.

And dammit, my head is on straight.

I'm not my family.

I'm not my sister.

I'm not Lucas's parents.

I'm my own person, and I can choose to love in my own way.

I raise my face, wipe the tears, and speak from my heart. "I don't want a halfway love. I don't want the middle ground. I want all of Lucas—the friendship and the connection and the sex and the love and the French fries."

Amy scoffs playfully. "Well, always say yes to the French fries."

But there's something I need to say no to.

Something I need to kick to the curb.

My fear.

It's time to shed that bitch.

28

LUCAS

The voice grates on my ears.

She's too cheery.

Too happy.

Too much everything.

"And then he said, 'Well, can I get you some coconut whipped cream?' And I was like, 'Did I hit the jackpot or what?'"

I grit my teeth, willing the blonde at the table next to me to stop talking on FaceTime.

But no such luck.

"Cha-ching! You hit triple cherries," her friend says at the decibels of a jet engine.

The woman points at her on the screen. "He hit the triple cherry."

I groan at the terrible pun, my annoyance meter reaching one thousand as I try to review this client pitch while the ladies make bawdy jokes about cherries.

The meter is about to run higher, because out of the corner of my eye, I see the blonde stand, glance around, and head straight for Reid and me.

"Hey, can you just watch my—"

"No," I bite out. I don't even look her way.

She holds up her hands in surrender. "Oh, okay, sorry."

"Forgive him," Reid says. "He knows not what he's done. He's having a bad week. We'd be happy to watch it. Especially for a pregnant woman."

I snap my gaze back to the blonde. Whoa. She has a basketball in her belly.

"Are you sure?" she asks Reid.

"Positive. My mate simply has his pants in a twist because he's in love with a woman and can't man up and tell her."

The pregnant woman laughs. "You should just tell her, sweetie."

I stare at Reid, my eyes narrowed to slits. "Seriously?"

"Yes, I'm serious."

The woman holds up a finger. "I'll be right back, and then I want to hear all about this." She dashes off to the restroom.

I huff. "No, I meant did you seriously need to tell her?"

"Yes, I did. Because someone needs to tell you. Oh, wait, let me do it." He squares his shoulders, clears his throat, and forms a megaphone with his hands around his mouth. "Get your head out of your arse."

I stare at him, unblinking. We're two cats, facing off. I cast about for a snarky reply. Search for a smart-aleck remark. But I've got nothing.

I just shrug.

"So it *is* that bad," Reid remarks.

"What do you mean?"

"You have it so bad that you have no fight left in you." He heaves a sigh. "You're a mess."

"Yes. I am definitely a mess," I concede.

A mess of sadness. A mess of frustration. A mess of missing and longing and wanting.

Seconds later, the woman waddles back, pulls up a chair, and says, "I'm Meg. I'm eight months pregnant. Tell me everything."

Reid smiles and extends a hand. "I'm Reid. Pleasure to meet you. This is Lucas. See his face? It's a sad face. Why is Lucas sad? Because poor Lucas suffers from a pathetic condition known as pigheadedness. It's preventing him from telling the woman he spent last weekend with that he doesn't want to be just friends. That he wants to be with her literally all the time. And do you know the side effect of this condition?"

"What is it?" Meg asks, enrapt.

Reid taps his chest. "He's infecting me with his negative mood. I'm an hour away from binge-watching tear-jerkers and drowning my sorrows in Ben and Jerry's."

Meg turns to me, frowning. "You shouldn't infect your friend. You should talk to this woman you met."

"I didn't just meet her. I knew her ten years ago," I correct her. Facts are facts, and they need to be laid out.

"We were great friends. The best of friends back then. And I was falling hard for her. But I said some stupid things, and we never made up, and we became enemies over the years. And then this weekend . . ."

I take a beat as the memories of the weekend, still so damn potent, flood my mind and spread through all the molecules in my body. "We spent an amazing weekend together. Well, it was twenty-four hours, but I just knew . . . I knew," I say, my heart crawling up into my throat again.

Meg's eyes widen. "You knew that you wanted another chance?"

I nod. "Yes," I say, laying it all out there for a perfect stranger and my best friend.

"A second chance at love? And you're sitting here sad instead of telling her the truth of your heart?" Her question is simple.

And maybe that's why it jars me.

It knocks me out of my funk.

My horrible mood caused by a terrible case of falling in love and burying that feeling like an ostrich shoving its head in the sand.

I've been denying everything, ignoring everything, and forcing my feelings into a box, closing the lid and hiding it in a corner of the attic where it'll be buried for years again if I don't open it.

Wait. That's wrong.

More like a lifetime.

And that's not a way to live.

I stand. "No. I'm *not* sitting here." I stab my finger against the table. "I'm not sitting here another damn minute. You know why?" I ask, suddenly emboldened. Because in the grand scheme of things, the last few days without her is the blink of an eye. It's nothing. But we've veered down this road before. And no way am I taking ten more years to find my way back to her.

Fuck adulting.

Because this? This is adulting.

Deciding.

Right here, right now, I'm deciding to do love differently.

Love might be dangerous, but not loving is deadly.

I'll take my chances. Because Lola is worth it.

"Why?" Meg asks, returning to my question.

"Because I fell in love with Lola ten years ago, and I never told her. And I lost her. I'm not losing her again." I hold out my arms wide. "It's that simple." And when I say it, something loosens in me. Not a weight, but a knot. A knot of frustration at the world, at people, at the way things don't work out. I turn to Meg. "I'm sorry I was rude about not watching your laptop. I get it. You had to pee. It's all good." I turn to Reid. "And I'm sorry I'm a dick sometimes."

"Sometimes?" he asks with a laugh.

"A lot," I correct.

He waves it off. "You're a good one, mate."

I turn to the pregnant woman again. "I think it's great that your husband gets you coconut whipped cream. I have someone I want to do that for, and I can't wait to tell her."

Reid cuts in, raising a hand. "But don't you have to go make that presentation at the awards ceremony?"

I smile. "As a matter of fact, I do."

29

LOLA

The thing about being the responsible one is just that—responsibility weighs on you.

It nags you.

It tells you to head downtown to the hotel where the Design-Off event is held, bring your laptop, and have your pitch ready.

I'm wearing a blue pencil skirt, a white short-sleeve blouse, and polka-dot heels.

I'm professional but artsy.

It's perfect for the presentation I have to give, right before Lucas's slot.

It's perfect to wear as I share my vision with experts in my field.

It's perfect for being the responsible one.

I have a plan. Present, wait, and then grab that man and tell him how I feel.

But here's the other thing.

Hearts have a mind of their own.

Because when I arrive at the Luxe Hotel, I don't listen to my head. I listen to my heart.

And my heart says *he's here.*

He's waiting for me outside the building, looking cool and gorgeous in a charcoal suit with a crisp white shirt and no tie. His hair is messy, like it usually is, and the most delicious amount of stubble lines his jaw.

Slamming the door of the cab, I hoist my purse with my laptop in it higher on my shoulder, and I walk.

To him.

To possibility.

To a chance.

Not just a second chance, but a terrifying and thrilling chance at love. The very thing that has taunted me my whole life.

The demon I've hidden from.

The monster I've avoided.

But love can be so much more than that.

It can fill your heart and mind with so much incomparable joy. And joy is what I feel. Not a shred of responsibility. Not an ounce of doubt.

As I walk to him, he walks to me. A knowing grin is on his face. There's a gleam in his chocolate eyes. A passion. An intensity that's all his, and all mine, and all ours.

We reach each other at the same time.

"Lola," he says, speaking first. "Do you want to know the whole truth of ten years ago?"

I stop, startled. I wasn't expecting that twist. "Yes, I do."

He takes a breath, steps closer, and cups my cheek. His hand is so warm, so right.

"The reason it hurt? The reason it all went to hell so quickly?"

"Yes?" I ask, my voice pitched with worry but also hope.

His eyes lock with mine like he never wants to look away from me. "I was falling in love with you."

I gasp, bringing my hand to my mouth as tears fill my eyes. I'm not a crier, but for the second time today, a lump fills my throat. "You were?"

He nods, his expression so earnest, so true. "I was falling so damn hard for you, and then everything combusted. And I was petrified. I'd been falling in love with you, and then I just lost you. I can blame my family for my fear of love. But I have myself to blame too. I hated losing you, but I didn't know how to fight for you. And the end result was that, in my mind, love equaled pain."

My lips quiver, and I nod, understanding him even more now. I lift a hand and touch his arm, needing contact. "I was falling in love with you too," I say, and that admission feels like a new kind of freedom as all the secrets of the past tumble free.

His lips crook into a grin. "Is that so?"

"That's why I couldn't bear to just be friends with you. I wanted more. I wanted it all with you. I didn't know how to have it. But Lucas," I say, taking a breath, drawing more strength, "that's the reason I've never fallen for anyone else."

"It is?"

"I gave my heart to you a long time ago. No one else could ever come close."

He groans his appreciation, a warm, sexy sound. Then his fingers thread into my hair. "Know what I think?"

"What do you think?" I ask, unable to mask a grin.

"That no one should come between us again. You're the one, Lola. You're the one who got away. You're the one I want back. You're the one I love."

My heart soars, flying free, taking off into the sky, rising to the stars. A wish that has come true. This moment is almost too much, but I want to savor every second of the recklessness, the risk.

I rise up, press my lips to his, and whisper my deepest fear and my greatest joy: "I'm in love with you too."

He doesn't let me go. He kisses me tenderly.

He kisses me like we have years to make up for. Like I'm the one he wants to kiss tonight and tomorrow and for all time.

As his lips explore mine, my head goes hazy, my body floods with endorphins. Tingles spread down my arms, across my skin, everywhere.

We kiss like there's nothing else in the world but us, our lips, our touch. Like the city's millions can walk on by, the night can carry on, and we'll do the same. We'll carry on with each other.

When we break the kiss, he looks woozy and ridiculously happy.

Like how I feel.

And I feel something else too.

Something wild and daring.

Something reckless.

There's a crazy beating in my heart as an idea takes hold. An idea that won't let go. This is something my sister would do.

And maybe that's not such a bad thing. Maybe I can learn from the reckless one.

I dance my fingers up the buttons on his shirt. "What would you say about screwing the awards?" I whisper, like we're scofflaws, breaking all the rules. "Let's be the irresponsible ones."

His grin says yes. "How about sex, bowling, and French fries?"

"I'd sell my soul for that."

He draws me close. "But you don't have to. All you have to do is let me love you as so much more than a friend."

"Consider it done."

30

LUCAS

It's safe to say neither one of us is going to win.

It's also safe to say neither one of us cares.

Later that night, after round two, I grab my buzzing phone and check my email.

It's from the competition organizers.

"Oops," I say when I read it. "Turns out we were disqualified on account of *not showing up*."

She laughs as she shrugs. "Win some. Lose some. Win some more," she says, then drops a kiss on my lips.

Yep. I won.

I won big.

And later that night, she wins when I take her bowling at Pin-Up Lanes.

She crushes me.

But in my defense, I can't stop touching her, kissing her, wrapping my arms around her. I have years to make up for. And I plan on doing just that.

After the game, we indulge in fries.

"It was one week ago when we were here," she says, glancing around.

"Who would have thought twenty-four hours would change everything?" I muse.

She takes a bite of another fry, and when she's done, she lifts her chin, a quizzical look in her eyes. "Do you think you can fall in love in twenty-four hours?"

I shake my head.

Her brow furrows. "You don't think so?"

I lean across the table and press a kiss to her lush lips. "I don't think so. I *know so.*"

When we leave, we pass the counter, and the guy in the vest snaps his gaze to us. "Hey! How did it all work out?"

"We gathered all their things," I say. "Got it all sorted out."

"That's great," he says, but then he makes a rolling gesture. "I mean the other thing. The thing Harrison was working on?"

Lola's brow creases. "That *was* it. The scavenger hunt thing?"

The man's expression falls, and he waves a hand. "Never mind."

But something else is going on. "What should we 'never mind'?" I ask.

The guy shakes his hand. "I'm sure it's nothing. Just a crazy idea."

Lola tilts her head and smiles. "Maybe tell us."

The man exhales sharply. "It's not my story to tell." He takes a beat. "It's sort of yours."

31

LOLA

I whip out my phone at lightning speed.

With guns blazing, I click open an email, ready to fire off a note to my sister's landlord.

But as Gmail auto-fills his address, a name blasts across my screen.

Amy.

I answer right away. Bowling pins clang on the hardwood from a nearby game.

"Hey, what's up?"

"Remember that exclusive submission? The one I was meeting the agent about on Sunday night?"

"Sure," I say, recalling what she'd told me. "The comedy, right?"

"It arrived this morning. I read most of it this afternoon. It's spectacular. Sarcastic, clever, original, and full of more heart than I ever expected. I want it badly, and if we get it, I want you to do the cover."

"That's great." Only, I doubt that's why she's calling on a Friday night. "But . . .?"

"There's no real 'but.' Well, except the ending. It needs a better one. I'm going to talk to the writer about fixing the ending," she says, excitement in her voice. "And a title change for sure. Talk about rambling. But the story felt somewhat familiar."

The hair on my arms stands on end, and Lucas shoots me a *what the hell is going on* look. "What do you mean, Amy? Is this bad?"

She laughs. "No, it's not bad. It's . . . interesting."

I pull Lucas aside, around the corner, down the hall, sharing the phone as Amy tells us about the novel she received.

It's not *The Happy-Go-Lucky Sadist.*

But it is written by him. He's not a TV writer anymore. He's writing books, and this one is called *That Time I Kicked Out the Love Birds, Bowled a Perfect Game, and Hung Out with the Llamas.*

32

HARRISON

What a difference quiet makes.

I stretch my arms and sigh contentedly, pleased with the last week of my life.

Is there anything better than conquering writer's block?

I think not.

Well, fine. Maybe one thing is better—conquering it like a motherfucking badass, because that's what I am. Judging from this late-night email from my agent telling me there's interest in my manuscript, that's exactly what I pulled off in a mere week.

I settle down into my couch, crack open a new can of orange soda, and set my feet on the coffee table.

Then I do my new favorite thing.

I listen.

To the sound of nothing.

Nada.

Zip.

It's heaven. A balm for the creative soul, and it's unleashed a torrent of ideas during the last seven days. A caper of sorts. A comedy. One man's journey to restore his faith in, well, himself.

Through cheese and bowling, pancakes and alpacas, and dance lessons.

That was unexpected. I never planned to take tango lessons. But I can't seem to stop taking them.

Or to stop seeing—

Buzz.

What is that godforsaken infernal noise?

Oh, right.

The buzzer.

I heave myself up, head to the intercom, and ask who's there.

"Lola and Lucas."

Not gonna lie. That delights me. Those two are fascinating. Inspiring too. "As they say on *The Price is Right*, come on up. Well, it's 'come on down,' but you get the gist."

I open the door to wait for them, and a minute later, the pair of riddlers strides toward me down the hall, curious looks on their faces.

"Hey," Lucas says, then extends a hand. "I'm Lucas."

"I feel like I know you already," I say.

"And you do, in many ways," he says.

The dark-haired woman offers her hand, and we shake. "Weirdly, it's a pleasure to meet you," she says.

"Weirdly, indeed." I invite them in, and they follow my lead, heading inside.

Lucas tilts his head, then scratches his jaw. "So, you wrote a book about that wild-goose chase you sent us on?"

I hold my arms out wide. "Screw that one-month novel-writing camp. I wrote it in five days. Top that!"

Lola laughs. "Can't beat that." But then her expression turns more serious. "But I want to know something. Was that whole breakup letter to Luna and Rowan designed to get us together?" She points from herself to Lucas. "Since I'm presuming you heard about us during their many fights?"

A laugh bursts from my chest. Are they for real? They think I'm a matchmaker? "Are you kidding?"

"No. I'm serious," Lola says, her lips ruler-straight, her eyes intense.

"Did you actually read the story?"

She shakes her head.

"One, it's not a love story. Two, it's not about the two of you. And three, why the hell would I try to get you two together?"

"As a novel idea?" Lucas offers.

I laugh again, louder, deeper this time. "Take a good look at the man in front of you." I hold out my arms and turn in a slow circle. "Do I look like cupid? Do you see wings? A bow and arrow? A *diaper*?"

Lola has the good sense to look sheepish. "Obviously not."

I tap my chest. "I'm not a secret matchmaker. I'm not any sort of matchmaker. Plus, happy endings are unnecessary. The guy doesn't always get the girl, because he doesn't need the girl." I raise my chin. "My book is a personal journey. A comedy about a man figuring out what he wants in life. His happiness. Not happiness with another person. I don't need to have lovers smooching at the end."

They laugh, and Lola wraps an arm around Lucas. "Well, thanks anyway. That was an accidental by-product, then, of that time you kicked out the Love Birds."

"Wait. You two got back together?" I ask with a groan.

Lucas drops a kiss to her cheek. "We did. So, thanks, even though you didn't mean to do that."

I drop my face in my hands. "That was never the goal," I grumble.

"What was the goal?"

I raise my face. "It was for me. It was the first time I was inspired in ages. I wrote about a man finding his place in the world."

"Through a breakup letter to his noisy tenants?"

"Yes. It was restorative. It was everything I needed. I had no idea when I wrote that letter. I wrote it for payback, but as soon as I started dropping off their things, it unlocked my story. I wrote, and I wrote, and I wrote."

"Good," Lucas says with a grin. "Looks like it worked out for all of us." He turns to leave but stops and swings back. "One more thing. How did the dance lessons work out?"

My traitorous heart hammers as I picture Angeline, the captivating, clever dance instructor who taught me the first steps of tango. Whom I invited to dinner. Whom I saw tonight.

Whom I'll see tomorrow. "They're working out great."

Lola lifts a brow. "Maybe that's your ending."

I sneer. "Books don't need happy endings."

"No, but sometimes life is better with them," she says, then waves goodbye. "Thanks again. Perhaps you do have a touch of cupid in you."

They turn and leave, holding hands.

Something in me burns with annoyance.

I'm not the guy who writes romance.

I don't believe in it.

But when I return to my couch and find a message from Angeline telling me she's looking forward to tomorrow's dance lesson, maybe, just maybe, I wouldn't mind a happier ending for me.

LOLA

A few months later

Angeline was right.

Lucas and I rock at tango.

We take lessons a few times a month.

And when we finish tonight's lesson with a flourish and a dip, Angeline claps. "Bravo! You're fantastic."

Lucas offers a hand and pulls me up. "You are fantastic," he says to me.

Angeline strides over to us and sets a hand on his shoulder, then mine. "I told you, you had couple's energy. I was right."

"You do have crazy lovebird energy!" That's Rowan, chiming in from the other side of the studio.

"Yes! They have so much of it that it's like a new perfume," Luna chirps.

I roll my eyes, but they're right. Those two lovebirds are definitely right. And even though they didn't try to bring us back together, they're happy as clams that we are.

We are too.

So happy, in fact, that sometimes the four of us take dance lessons together.

But we make sure to schedule them when Harrison isn't coming by to see his girlfriend.

After all, there's no need for Luna and Rowan to bump into the enemy, even though he's not truly the enemy.

Better safe than sorry.

We say goodbye to Angeline and take off into the Manhattan night to grab a bite with our siblings.

Over sandwiches and salads, we catch up on the latest news from the Love Birds tour, and get the details about their new place in Queens.

Lucas lifts a fry, pointing it at Rowan. "You better be quiet in your new apartment. I don't want to do another wild-goose chase."

Rowan smirks. "But maybe you do?"

Luna squeezes Rowan's arm and plants a kiss on his cheek. "I'm sure they do. They loved it. It brought them together."

Lucas rolls his eyes, but simply shrugs.

It did bring us together, and I'd go on countless more with this man.

* * *

A few more months later

Our friends keep us busy with weddings.

We go to Amy and Linc's ceremony in a park, where they read passages to each other from some of their favorite books. Then Tristan and Peyton celebrate in a gorgeous room at the Luxe Hotel, where Tristan's brother is the best man and the bride looks more beautiful than she's ever looked.

We dance and laugh and toast.

And when the weddings are done, we go home with each other, since we made the jump and now live together.

We're sometimes irresponsible, and truth be told, I *might not* do a damn thing about being outrageously loud when Lucas takes me to new heights of pleasure every night.

But the walls are thick, and there are no complaints from neighbors. Or landlords.

Speaking of landlords . . . one afternoon, Lucas and I pop into An Open Book to pick up copies of *That Time I Kicked Out the Lovebirds.*

Amy asked Harrison to shorten the title, and he agreed it made sense.

She asked him, too, for a better ending, and though he grumbled, he added in a closing coda where the guy falls for his tango instructor.

Whether it's art imitating life or life imitating art is anyone's guess.

But inarguably it's a damn good ending for his story.

I tap the cover—a fun illustrated design of a New York apartment stoop with guitars and notebooks strewn across it. Lucas and I designed it together.

When I flip open the page, I grin at the dedication.

To Lucas and Lola. I do not have a cupid in me at all, and we will never agree on that. But it does take two to tango, so thanks for that.

It's fitting and so perfectly him.

After we purchase the books, we leave, heading for the train station, and I tell Lucas about my new clients. My firm is growing, even without an award to my credit. Peter remains a top client, and his YouTube channel's popularity has soared. So has his love life with his new lady blader, and they make videos together sometimes.

Lucas and Reid moved into their office space at last, and that makes my man happier. He was never one for coffee shops, though he does offer a toast to a gal named Meg every time we grab a cup at Doctor Insomnia's.

Life is good.

Love is wonderful.

And llamas and alpacas are even better on the afternoon we spend tending to the cousins at the sanctuary.

When we leave, Lucas stops at the barn door. "Hold on. I dropped something."

I spin around to find him on one knee. I blink, surprise whipping through me as the man I love holds out a blue velvet box.

His brown eyes hold mine fiercely. "Lola Dumont, this is where I knew I was falling in love with you a second time around. In this place, we talked about halfway love, and that's when I was certain, even though I didn't know it at the time, that I wanted *everything* with you. It took me a few days to figure it out, but since I have, I've never looked back. And I only want to keep moving forward with you."

My heart expands. My skin tingles. And I feel like I'm glowing all over.

"Will you marry me?" he asks.

I grin like an alpaca as I fall to my knees, joining him, letting him slide a gorgeous diamond on my finger.

I say yes to him, yes to love, yes to forever.

The next year, we're married here at the farm. We ask for donations to the sanctuary instead of gifts, and Davina serves as our justice of the peace.

Frick and Frack are in attendance too, wearing bow ties.

And Lucas is still a little bit in love with them. And I'm all the way in love with him. There is nothing halfway about our love, or how we dance the tango for our first song.

THE END

Ready for more romance and adventure? I can not wait to share **PS IT'S ALWAYS BEEN YOU** with all my fabulous readers! Don't miss this epic romance! Preorder now!

A sweeping, second chance romance from #1 NYT Bestseller Lauren Blakely that weaves mystery, passion, and humor as two present-day lovers search for a love story from the past...

Past loves should stay in the past.

After the way my first love took off for the ends of the earth, the last thing I want is to see him on billboards and bookstore bestseller shelves. Now my boss just handed me the project that could make my career. All I have to do is partner up with the man, the myth, the legend—adventurer Hunter Armstrong.

That's easier said than done, because when we reconnect I learn Hunter has his own agenda on this project. And it's not to find a treasure in art and antiques. It's me. But what we discover shocks both of us and we have no choice but to follow the clues....

Preorder now!

ALSO BY LAUREN BLAKELY

FULL PACKAGE, the #1 New York Times Bestselling romantic comedy!

BIG ROCK, the hit New York Times Bestselling standalone romantic comedy!

THE SEXY ONE, a New York Times Bestselling standalone romance!

THE KNOCKED UP PLAN, a multi-week USA Today and Amazon Charts Bestselling standalone romance!

MOST VALUABLE PLAYBOY, a sexy multi-week USA Today Bestselling sports romance! And its companion sports romance, MOST LIKELY TO SCORE!

WANDERLUST, a USA Today Bestselling contemporary romance!

COME AS YOU ARE, a Wall Street Journal and multi-week USA Today Bestselling contemporary romance!

PART-TIME LOVER, a multi-week USA Today Bestselling contemporary romance!

UNBREAK MY HEART, an emotional second chance USA Today Bestselling contemporary romance!

BEST LAID PLANS, a sexy friends-to-lovers USA Today Bestselling romance!

The Heartbreakers! The USA Today and WSJ Bestselling rock star series of standalone!

CONTACT

I love hearing from readers! You can find me on Twitter at LaurenBlakely3, Instagram at LaurenBlakelyBooks, Facebook at LaurenBlakelyBooks, or online at LaurenBlakely.com. You can also email me at laurenblakelybooks@gmail.com

Made in the USA
San Bernardino, CA
24 February 2020